Walk On

Other books by Nan Evenson

Good Night (Not Really):
Let's Count Forward AND Backward

It's a Terrible Day (Not Really):
Let's Count by Twos

Walk On

Nan Evenson

atmosphere press

© 2025 Nan Evenson

Published by Atmosphere Press

Cover design by Felipe Betim

No part of this book may be reproduced without permission from the author except in brief quotations and in reviews. This is a work of historical fiction, based on real events. However, some artistic license has been taken to move the story forward.

Atmospherepress.com

For those who walked the
Trail of Tears,
You are not forgotten.

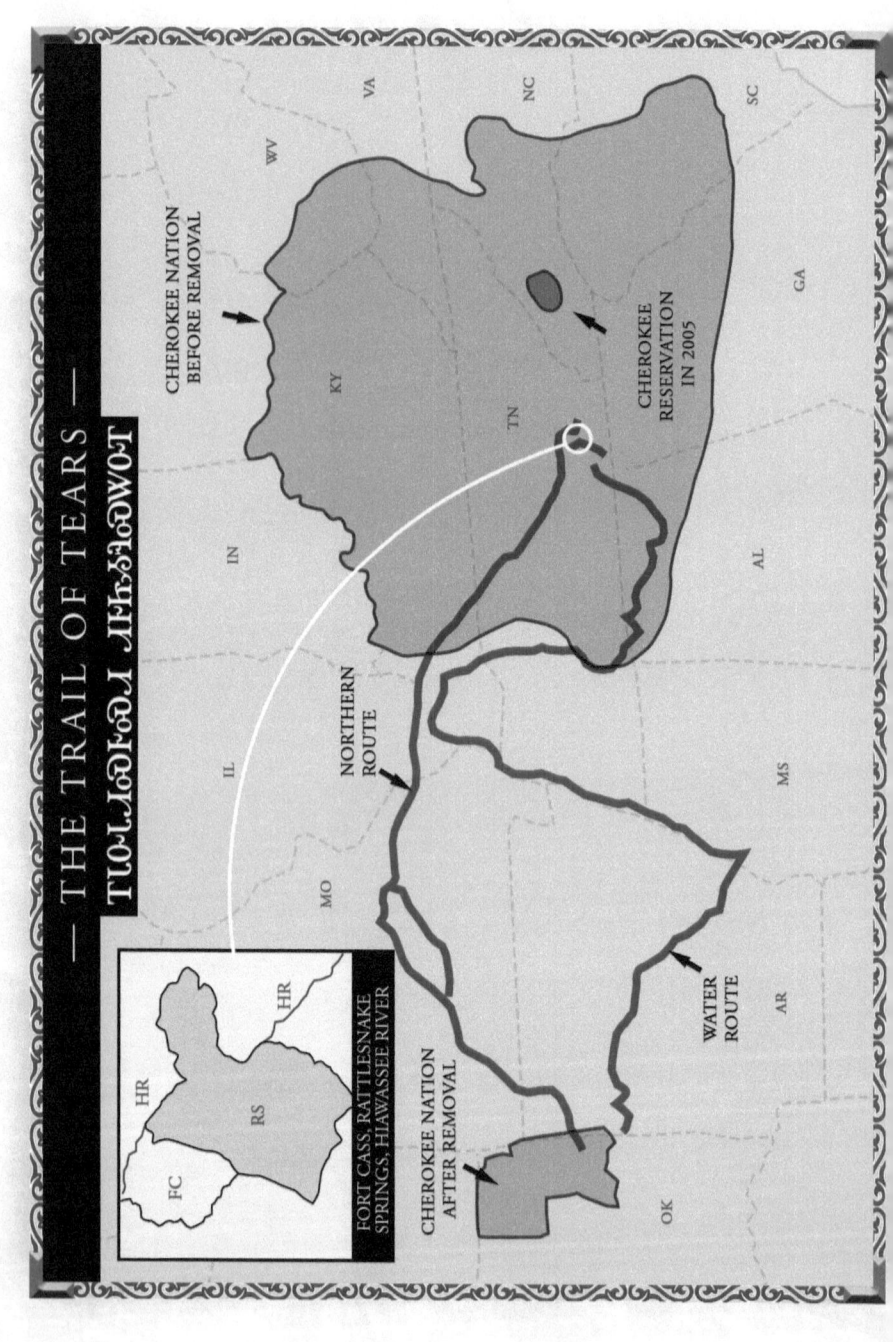

Author's Note

I believe there are good and bad people everywhere and that history is complicated and messy. I didn't want to write a book that simplified this important event, The Trail of Tears. This book is about people who carried out the tragedy and those who tried to stop it. I want readers to know about those who walked that terrible trail but not only about the people who were lost. We also need to remember those who came out of the wreckage and walked on.

– 1 –

Snakes

At the end of this crisp October day, Callie filed out of the one-room schoolhouse with the other students at Fort Cass. It was hard to stay in line, though, because instead of heading home right away, she decided to visit her friend Mohe at the horse corral. It wasn't a long walk, but it was a pretty one. Orange and red leaves scattered as she jumped and kicked her way through them.

Fort Cass, Tennessee, was a mile to the west of Rattlesnake Springs, a grouping of thirteen Cherokee villages. Callie's was the nearest to the fort, and her walk took her along the shore of the deep and fast-running Hiawassee River. The nearest town, Charleston, was a mile to the east. White farmers were sprinkled throughout the land. The sprawling Fort Cass, grandly centered between the Cherokee people and the townspeople and farmers, kept them apart but also brought them together for trade deals.

As different as these groups of people were, they all depended on the mighty Hiawassee River for water and fish. The blue-brown shimmering waters snaked through their lives. The fort had been set up in 1819 before Callie was born as a kind of embassy for the United States government to keep an eye on the Cherokee people who lived in the area as well as to trade with them. Now, nearly twenty years later, in 1838, the generally peaceful relationship had begun to change into something much darker.

Callie knew to approach quietly and not spook the horses stabled in the corral at the edge of her village. Mohe's back was to her, and his broadening shoulders made him look more than three years older than Callie's fourteen years. His job guarding the horses was an important one. The Cherokee people were proud of their animal friends, and she knew of many horses lovingly passed down from father to son. Horses made people's lives easier and brought them happiness. For special ceremonies, their owners painted beautiful designs on the animals' graceful necks with red and blue berry juices. An angry voice interrupted her daydreaming, causing her to duck behind a corral wall.

"Damn it! Lost a shoe and now you're lame. What good are ya to me if ya can't walk!"

A sudden gunshot rang out, and a flock of sparrows in a nearby tree flew away in unison. Callie peeked around the corner to see a tall, sharp-chinned white man dressed in a ragged, dusty, blue soldier's uniform. A small, light brown horse had dropped onto the dry weeds with a heavy thud. Callie had seen lame Cherokee horses shot if they were unable to walk, but it had been done with care for the animal. This horse had been shot without any kindness, without a tender word or a reassuring pat on the nose. Shock burned through her.

Next, a wave of sadness rocked her. Callie lowered her head, fighting back tears, her long, black braids swinging forward. She shivered in her calf-length deerskin dress, fidgeting with the belt at her waist. The thick strip of soft, brown leather felt soothing. She took a deep breath and flattened herself against one of the three corral walls. The fourth side had no wall but was enclosed by the sturdy pine-rail fence Mohe sat on. It had been unusually warm earlier that day when she had been in school, but now the sun hung low in the sky behind the rolling blue-green hills. She wished she were home at her Grandmother Ama's hut, sitting by the warm fire.

Callie watched as Mohe, whose name meant "the elk," walked toward the white man. He must have witnessed the shooting from his perch on the corral's fence. He quietly asked the white man as he walked toward him, "She yours?"

"She was," the man snapped. "But she ain't nobody's now. Give me your best horse."

"I do not understand," said Mohe cautiously, jumping to the ground with surprising grace.

His well-worn, caramel-colored deerskin boots were decorated with deep blue and creamy white beads. A necklace of leather and three bear claws lay across his gray cotton shirt. A brown cloth band held back his black, shoulder-length hair. He pulled the fringed, sand-colored wool blanket tighter around his shoulders. As Callie watched, she tugged at the blue shawl around her shoulders too. The man's voice felt like sharp winter's ice. His hair reminded her of short, brittle brown wheat, unlike the long, sleek black hair of the men in her tribe.

"Do you understand this, then?" the man said, as he spat on the ground. He waved his large flintlock pistol toward the herd of about thirty horses who were shuffling around nervously after the loud bang. When his gaze landed on a muscled Appaloosa mare, a scruffy white female with big brown spots on her back and legs, he put the gun in the holster at his side. Smaller brown spots covered the rest of her, and freckles splashed across her nose. Her name was Shiko Waka, or Big Dog, and she belonged to Mohe.

The soldier opened the gate, stepped inside the corral, carrying the bridle attached to the reins he had taken off his horse before he shot her. He pushed the other horses aside as he made his way to Big Dog. When he got to her, he threw the reins around her neck and tried to shove the steel bit into her mouth so that he could direct her movements. She threw her head back to avoid his aggression, but he grabbed her by her thick white mane and jammed the bit in. Callie knew that's not how a horse should be treated and that Big Dog was not used to the bit. She wanted to help Big Dog and Mohe, but stayed hidden out of fear.

The tall man yanked on the reins and led the skittish animal out of the corral. Big Dog hesitated when she saw the dead horse, so he pulled harder. A thick wool saddle blanket with wide stripes of blue, black, and red on a tan background was draped over the fence. The soldier threw it over her broad back. Then, he stepped on the reins so that she couldn't move while he threw the heavy, plain brown leather saddle he'd taken off his horse on top of the blanket. She pranced from side to side to get away from him. He kneed her hard in the gut.

Mohe watched in complete stillness, his facial expression seething with helplessness and rage. The man mounted Big Dog and rode off without a word, jerking and steering his new horse, Mohe's friend, around the dead horse. He kicked Big Dog with the sharp-edged spurs attached to his knee-high, black military boots.

Callie stood where she was, unable to lift her feet. This man was not one for kindness in any sense of the word. If horses or people were in his way, she knew they paid the price. After she lost sight of the man, she left her hiding place and ran straight into Mohe's arms. He was shaking, but not from the cold.

"Callie, did you see that? You must tell no one what happened. For now. I need to think about what to do. Do you promise? Do you?" Mohe begged her in the singsong tempo of the Cherokee language.

"Who was that man? Will Shiko Waka be safe?" she asked, breathing hard.

"I don't know. I need time to think," he said, more impatient than before.

She went on, her voice rising. "He can't do that! He can't just take her! You need to go to the fort and tell the general about this! And I need to tell Waya!" She watched for his reaction.

"Tell the general? Tell him? He does nothing for us. He doesn't care about a Cherokee horse being stolen. I told you, please, speak to no one and let me think. Promise you will not tell your uncle. Even though Waya is our tribe's leader, I need to decide what to do."

She looked into his angry, frightened eyes and blurted out, "All right. I won't tell anyone!" She turned away and ran as fast as her long, strong legs could carry her to the safety of her Grandmother Ama's and Uncle Waya's hut.

Callie wished she could forget what had happened that afternoon. Her day had started out beautifully at Fort Cass's one-room schoolhouse. She was the only Cherokee student in attendance, and as usual, she learned and played along with the other twelve children from the fort, ages six to fourteen. A handful of senior-level officers had been allowed to bring their wives and children to live with them at the fort. Katherine Miller was their teacher, and her husband, Lieutenant General Thomas Miller, reported to the highest-ranking officer at the fort, General Winfield Scott. The children of the soldiers were used to the polite, curious Cherokee children wandering in and out of school whenever it appealed to them.

Callie had started attending ten months earlier and went about once per week. She liked school at the fort. Even though she'd never had formal schooling in Rattlesnake Springs, Callie had been taught practical skills, including farming and and taking care of her home. She developed a deep spirituality as well as respect for the earth and for all life, which served her well in everyday life. Callie knew that the Cherokee leader, Sequoya, had created an alphabet for their language, but she hadn't learned it yet.

"Good morning, Callie. I'm glad you're here today. Come

in, and we'll practice reading,"

Katherine said as she picked up a bowl of red-and-white striped hard candies.

"Everyone gets candy today!" she said, smiling at Callie. The children, who were already squirming in their seats, couldn't restrain themselves anymore. They flooded toward their teacher with outstretched hands.

"Guests first. Callie?" she asked. Katherine had light brown hair pulled back in a loose bun. She wore a white apron every day, tied at the waist and hanging nearly to the ground over her floor-length dress. Today's light green dress accented her slight frame. She didn't wear the standard fluffy petticoat that usually filled out women's dresses, because she said it was too big and got in the way of her hugging the children.

Callie stepped forward confidently and took a candy while nodding slightly at Katherine to thank her. The students now lined up in age order as was their custom. The oldest two students in line were boys, the Millers' fourteen-year-old son, Jameson, and his twelve-year-old friend, George. Jameson was tall and lean with deep blue eyes and blond hair that didn't respect a good brushing. He was always in motion. George, small for his age, had red, curly hair inherited from his Irish father. When people commented on his hair and bright green eyes set against his pale skin, George frowned.

Katherine winked at her son when it was his turn. Callie watched him pick out his candy, and when Jameson turned to go back to his seat, they glanced at each other. She smiled at him, not caring that her teeth were crooked.

She looked different to the students, but by now they were used to her fringed deerskin dress and moccasin boots, toes covered in red beads that made little clicking noises when she walked. Katherine divided the students into three groups, each group with different assignments, depending on age and skill level. While the students were studying, Katherine took Callie aside.

"How is your grandmother?"

"She is good. She make cornbread for you." Callie pulled a chunk of yellow bread wrapped in a cornhusk from a large leather pouch hanging from a deer-hide strap. It was slung over her left shoulder across her chest. Although Callie understood many words in English, she made speaking errors. It was especially difficult for her to get verb tenses correct. Sometimes Katherine corrected her, and sometimes she didn't. She had told Callie the most important thing was to try speaking and not worry about the rightness of it. For example, "make" and "made" sounded alike to Callie, and if people understood her, she had no desire to be perfect.

"Please tell her thank you for me," said Katherine. "I miss your mother. Dove was such a special woman. It was an honor to help her learn some English at the school years ago. She was much quicker to pick it up than I was when she taught me some Cherokee words!"

Callie felt her stomach tighten and looked for a distraction. She picked up a bright red book that sat on the school's small, white wooden bookshelf. She loved to read, but this book was too difficult for her. Katherine gently took it from her and handed her another one with lots of pictures. Callie relaxed and Katherine led her to the youngest group of children, ages six to eight. Callie cheerfully joined the bouncy group, even though she towered over them.

Reading was at the center of the curriculum, along with writing, math, and useful skills. The students also learned to feed the horses, chickens, and pigs at the fort. They helped the soldiers tend the large, sprawling gardens full of healthy tomatoes, squash, corn, and beans, similar to what the Cherokee farmers grew. The girls learned to sew, and the boys practiced throwing stones at rabbits and deer who easily snuck into the loosely guarded fort to munch on the garden vegetables. The boys often missed, and the rabbits, especially, came back for seconds.

At lunchtime, the children tumbled outside to sit on the sunbaked, grassy area that had been matted down from their playing. Sometimes her Cherokee friend, Lula, came to school with Callie but not today. She felt George's eyes following her as she sat down alone on the ground. He adjusted his brown suspenders and shyly walked over to her.

"Callie, me and Jameson built us a hideaway in the woods. Do you want to see it sometime?"

"What is this 'hideaway'?" she asked, looking up at him.

"Just what it sounds like!" he said. "We made it out of logs and leaves like a little house, and it has three tree stumps in it for places to sit, and it's sort of hidden in the woods. We even have candles inside. You can stand full straight up in it!"

"Where is it?" she asked, tilting her head in curiosity.

"It's about ten minutes' walk from here, halfway between the fort and your village. Want to see it sometime? You can play a game of Graces with us, but I'll tell you what, Jameson is pretty darn good at that game."

Callie raised her eyebrows, and her golden-brown eyes found Jameson's blue eyes. He was also sitting on the ground about twenty feet away, eating his lunch. "May...be," she said. George blushed but got even braver. Noticing that she hadn't brought any lunch, he asked if she wanted some of his sandwich, hard wheat bread with dried strips of salty beef in it.

Carefully, she reached up and took the piece he had torn off. She smelled it before taking a bite. After a nibble, she spat it out with a small coughing noise. It was too salty and hard to chew. Although she knew about dried meat, this was different. Besides, she was used to eating freshly cooked meat. "Not good. Not good. Thank you."

Jameson, who had been watching them, laughed. Callie glanced at him sternly. He immediately stopped laughing and then ignored her. Jameson called out to George and asked if he wanted to move deeper into the tall grass to look for gophers and other small animals. George was always ready to look for what he called "critters."

As they walked away from the schoolhouse, Callie's eyes tracked the boys. She lost sight of them for a few minutes when she heard George yelling, "Help, help!"

Katherine ran toward the sound, but Callie was faster. Callie was thirty feet from the boys when she saw a large, coiled rattlesnake ready to strike George. The four-foot-long snake had a diamond-patterned back, and the rattle on its tail was making a loud, urgent, clacking noise. Jameson stood ten feet to the left of George, and both were frozen in place. They knew the slightest movement would cause the snake to attack.

Callie silently motioned to Katherine, who was behind her, to stop. Then, she carefully opened her leather pouch and pulled out a seven-inch-long knife with a light-colored, antler bone handle. Jameson stared as she very, very slowly lifted her right arm and, with quick force and accuracy, let the knife fly. It hit the body of the snake, and it collapsed to the ground, its rattle continuing to quake for some time. She put her knife back in its leather holster inside her large pouch.

"That gosh darn varmint almost bit me! Callie, you sure enough saved me!" said George as he shook out his legs.

Katherine rushed to the boy and gave him a hug while keeping a worried eye on her son who still hadn't moved. "Thank you, dearest Callie. You all get an extra piece of candy!"

As they walked back to the schoolhouse, Jameson casually took a few fast steps so that he could catch up to Callie. "Well, I guess you're pretty good with knives. I mean, I can throw one, too, of course. But it never hurts to learn more. Can you show me how to do that? You could come to our hideaway like George said."

Callie understood him but kept walking, ignoring him for a few seconds before responding, "May . . . be." She was distracted, thinking about going to the corral after school and telling Mohe all about the snake. She knew he would laugh at the story but also be impressed.

After leaving the corral that afternoon, the soldier galloped Big Dog toward the fort, using his small crop whip to make her go faster, striking her on her upper rear leg. She was not used to being whipped and jumped in a zigzag line to get away from the thin, razor-sharp piece of leather. He yanked at her bit which confused her even more. She whinnied and reared up slightly on her back legs. Holding on tightly to the saddle horn, he was surprised by and furious at this new horse and swore at her.

George and Jameson had played tag after school let out for the day. As they walked home, an out-of-control horse and its foul-mouthed rider nearly trampled them.

"Get out of the way, you dirty kids. Move!" shouted the man, as he struck Big Dog with the full force of his whip. The boys leapt out of the way, stunned, as he plowed past them.

"Where'd he get that pretty Cherokee horse?" whispered George as if he was afraid the man might turn and come back. "I know that soldier. His name is John Payne. My pa says he's mean as a snake."

"Well, I'd say your pa is sure right about that," said Jameson.

– 2 –
Songs

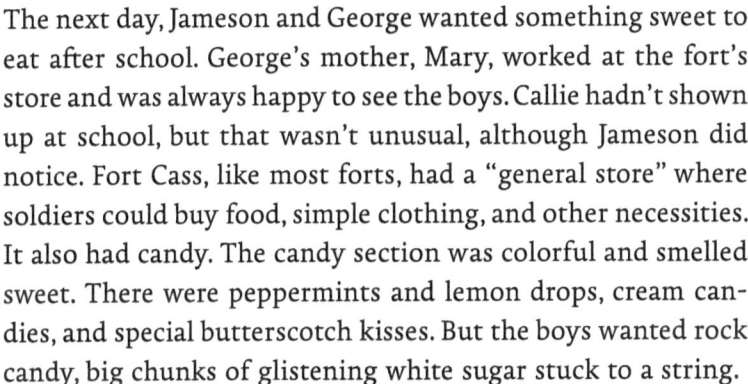

The next day, Jameson and George wanted something sweet to eat after school. George's mother, Mary, worked at the fort's store and was always happy to see the boys. Callie hadn't shown up at school, but that wasn't unusual, although Jameson did notice. Fort Cass, like most forts, had a "general store" where soldiers could buy food, simple clothing, and other necessities. It also had candy. The candy section was colorful and smelled sweet. There were peppermints and lemon drops, cream candies, and special butterscotch kisses. But the boys wanted rock candy, big chunks of glistening white sugar stuck to a string.

"How is your mother, Jameson?" Mary asked.

"Ma's fine. I'll tell her you asked about her," Jameson said.

"Me and Jameson would like some rock candies if we can. I mean . . . can we? Please, Ma?" asked George.

"It's Jameson and I, dear. If you boys bring me those gunny sacks of dry salted beef and potatoes sitting on the ground outside, I'll see what I have in the candy jar for you," she said with a smile, wiping her hands on the white apron that covered her long, light blue dress.

The boys nearly tripped over each other getting out the door. When they saw at least fifteen heavy sacks nearly as big as George, they balked. They had carried things for Mary before, but this was an unusually large shipment of supplies.

After a minute or two of staring at the sacks, Jameson figured candy would be worth it and picked up the end of the sack that looked smallest. George picked up the other end. Soon they had dragged all the gunny sacks up five stairs and into the store. She thanked them, and they each got a sugar rock string along with a bonus piece of licorice. While they were eating their treats, George begged to play with Jameson after dinner.

"Have you done your reading?" Mary asked.

"Yes, Ma."

"Oh, good. What is your book about, honey?"

"I don't rightly remember at this moment. I think it's a story about a bear. Yes, it's about a mean ol' bear."

"Let's have you get the book and read to me. That will be a nice break. And if there is time after you eat supper, take your bath, and practice some arithmetic, then you can play with Jameson," she said.

George trudged over to the small pile of school items that Mary kept at the store for him while she was working. He picked up a ragged copy of *Robinson Crusoe* by Daniel Defoe.

"Why, this isn't about a bear at all! I'm sure you got confused. It's about survival on an island. I think it's best you stay in tonight, so you can get some extra reading done. Begin, please," she said, sticking a knife into and ripping open one of the burlap bags of potatoes.

George made a "got caught" face at Jameson and started reading out loud. After ten long minutes, he said, "It's so awful dull, Ma."

Mary ignored his complaining and told him she was making rabbit stew for dinner. Jameson, who thought rabbit stew sounded pretty good, had something on his mind that he wanted to ask an adult.

"Mrs. Jones, I've heard talk of more soldiers coming to the fort. Is that why you have so many extra supplies?" He had been seeing more soldiers, many more, arrive every day.

"Yes, I believe more soldiers will be coming."

"They say they are going to make the Cherokee from Rattlesnake Springs move somewhere west so we can take their land. That's what I heard. Do you think that's why they're here?" asked Jameson.

"I can't say," she said, looking at the floor.

"Ma, we talked about that. Don't you remember?" said George.

Mary gave him a hard stare. George continued, "Pa says Senator Davy Crockett is the man to listen to on this whole dumb idea to move all the Cherokee people somewhere. Davy says that it has been Cherokee land for a long, long time, and now white men want it. Just so they can make a lot of money. And the Cherokee people have to go to land that is not as good for their farming. Seems to me and Davy that it's sure not our land. Seems to me we should all be friends."

"Boys, no more talk about this. George, say goodbye to Jameson and resume your reading," said Mary firmly.

"Bye," George said. He looked at Jameson and pinched his eyebrows together.

"Bye," said Jameson. As he walked out of the general store, he was hoping his mother would not make him read some boring book after supper. He had never thought much about the Cherokee in Rattlesnake Springs, but he was beginning to. He hoped the soldiers were coming in droves for any other reason than the one he feared was true.

Callie was looking forward to going to Mohe's home all day. He had invited her and some of the children for storytelling that night. He held story nights quite often, but tonight she wondered if he wanted to take his mind off the events of yesterday. After she finished her supper of squirrel stew with beans and wild onions, she swept up her five-year-old brother in her strong arms. "Let's go! Mohe has stories. Hurry!"

She threw a red blanket around him, hugged him tightly, and began to trot. In her haste, one of Little Wolf's small moccasins fell off, prompting him to yell out. "Stop, stop! My moccasin!"

She reluctantly turned back, sat him down on the trodden grass and slipped the soft leather shoe back onto his chubby foot. He ran after her as she skip-walked to Mohe's hut. The enormous orange harvest moon bathed Mohe's plain-looking hut in soft light that evening. His home was like most others in Rattlesnake Springs, built from large, wooden beams with river mud plastered between them to keep out the winter winds. The roof was made from the bark of red cedar trees that were nestled throughout the village.

Callie and her brother were the first to arrive. A fire warmed his home, the smoke escaping through a hole in the roof that could be covered with mats of leaves and branches. The familiar smell and sounds of crackling firewood welcomed them. There was a kitchen-sitting area, along with a sleeping area for Mohe and his mother. His father died in a hunting accident years before, and Callie knew he and his mother were close. Callie noticed it looked like Mohe hadn't slept all night.

Two more children popped in through the small door and greeted everyone. Lula was thirteen years old and a good friend of Callie's. She brought her three-year-old sister, Blossom, who was a little whiny, but calmed down when Lula whispered to her. Blossom crawled onto Lula's lap and was soon sucking her thumb contentedly. When the four children had finally settled cross-legged onto the bearskin rugs covering the ground, Mohe began. He spoke in hushed tones, making the children pay attention to his dreamlike, rhythmic voice.

"We will begin with the *Story of Fire*. Look hard at our own fire, which keeps us warm and cooks our food. You may take this for granted as if it has always been with our people. But that is not true."

"I'm looking at the fire! I'm looking right at it! See!" Little Wolf piped up.

Mohe smiled and continued. "The *Story of Fire* is old, and it is told from generation to generation. When time began, no one on earth had fire. Only the Thunders in the sky had it. The people begged them to send it to earth to help them, and finally, the Thunders sent down a beautiful fire. But it became stuck in a great sycamore tree. Five powerful animals tried to retrieve it, but they could not. Finally, the small and humble Water Spider was able to bring fire to our earth."

"I saw a spider yesterday! He was crawling up the wall!" said Little Wolf.

Callie playfully patted her brother on the head, messing up his thick, black hair. "That's nice, Little Wolf. I think the story is not really about a spider, though. It tells us we can all be strong. Is that right?"

Before Mohe could answer, Lula said, "I'm sure you are right, Callie. You're so smart. You always know what to do."

Mohe and Callie looked at each other, and a quick, invisible memory passed between them. She didn't always know what to do. Big Dog. *Where is she?* thought Callie. Mohe's jaw tightened, and he looked as though he could not think straight for a moment. The hut became still as the children noticed a change in the air. Even Blossom stopped sucking her thumb and looked up at Lula in confusion.

Mohe began again. Blossom clapped, and Mohe grinned at her.

"Here is the *Story of the Ballgame and the Animals*. There was to be a great and important ball game between all the animals. Some animals, such as the bear and turtle, tried to cheat at this game. But the birds were honest and good, and they won. Horses are honest and good too. My horse is the best friend I have ever had. You must always treat the animals, birds, and especially the horses, with care and gratitude."

Callie could see his pain but didn't know what to say.

After several more stories and lovely songs, Mohe said, "Now we are done, and you must go home to sleep. I wish good dreams for all of you."

Callie stood up with the others, but Mohe waved at her to sit back down. "Lula, will you and Blossom take Little Wolf back to his grandmother? I would like to talk with Callie alone."

As Lula took the boy's small hand in her left hand and Blossom's even smaller hand in her right, Little Wolf waved grandly and yelled an excited goodbye. Blossom kept sucking her thumb with her free hand. "Good night, sister! Good night, Mohe!" They tumbled out of the door.

"Yesterday a bad thing happened, and the evil spirit U-ya came. That soldier stole Big Dog, and I will never forgive him. I could not sleep last night and I have been thinking about it all day. My plan is to go into the fort tonight," he said.

"What do you want to do when you are there? It sounds so dangerous. You should wait and talk to my Uncle Waya. He can talk to other leaders too. They will know what to do," Callie said, biting her lip.

"I must go. I will make this right. No one else can help. A wrong like this cannot go without punishment. I will not find the man who did this, so I will kill the first soldier I come across, in vengeance." He clenched his jaw and looked away from her.

"What? What are you saying? This is wrong, and they will catch you. This is a terrible mistake! Maybe you should try to get Big Dog back instead of harming a soldier. There must be other ways!"

"It is no use. If I get her back, what is to stop that soldier, that evil U-ya, from taking my horse again and again? He stole my father's inheritance and my friend. You are young and you are strong but you are not a warrior. We must have revenge. You do not understand the ways of the men in our tribe, Callie. This must be. This will be," he said.

"Please, no. Maybe you can talk to General Scott, I think that is his name. At the fort, you can go there tomorrow and ask to speak with him. He will do justice," she said as her voice rose.

"I told you yesterday that man cares nothing for us. I have spoken with him before when I went with your uncle to try and stop this terrible thing they call 'removal.' We have tried to talk with him about it for two years, but the general does not listen. The American government wants to take our land, and they want us to walk away from it and go to another place that is not ours. He is not a man to do justice for the Cherokee people." Mohe spat on the ground.

"What? What do you mean, walk away?" she asked. She was anxiously twisting her braids.

"The way of 'wado,' peace, has no meaning for these men. Nothing touches their hearts. They will make us leave Rattlesnake Springs. They will force us west. And it will be soon."

"I don't understand. But you must not go to the soldiers' fort. It is too dangerous. Maybe you could talk to Mrs. Miller, the teacher at the fort?" said Callie, softening her voice.

But Mohe's voice rose. "She is a woman and controls nothing. Yes, she is good and has taught you English words, but her words don't matter to the white soldiers or to me. I will go."

Callie felt the power of an idea run up and down her body. "Then I will tell Grandmother Ama and Uncle Waya about your plan. They will stop you. And, even if you do not like this, I must try to keep you safe."

Mohe sat breathing heavily, staring at her. He tightened his fists. After a moment, he replied, "Yes, yes, you may be right. My plan is too dangerous. I should talk to Waya. I will think on it tonight."

Callie felt relieved and gave a little clap. "I am happy. I won't tell now because I know you will think the right way."

Callie almost pranced out of the hut. Her movements were always filled with a little bounce, but tonight she was floating.

She was proud to have persuaded Mohe because he could be stubborn and headstrong. As she strolled to her home at the edge of the village, she breathed in the cool air and hummed a lullaby her mother used to sing to her. It was a song about love and peace, and it had a steady beat like her mother's heartbeat when she held Callie close.

"Hey, yo, hey, yo ... Do you know I love you so?
I will never let you go.
To the stars and to the sky, you will always be my little love."

She didn't know, of course, that Mohe was singing a different song. It had a powerful unsteady rhythm. His was a song of revenge.

– 3 –

Earth

Callie felt sure she'd changed Mohe's mind and snuggled into her bearskin bed that night, but Mohe had not been swayed.

He snuck into Fort Cass not long after Callie left, his face painted with the specific colors warriors use when preparing for battle. Orange and red slashes ran down each cheek. He made no sound as he crept forward in his moccasin knee-high boots. Two guards sat at the large front gate on wooden three-legged stools. A small table, made from a tree stump, sat between them with a bottle of whiskey on the ground and cards scattered on top of the table.

The guards were drunk, swaying back and forth with their arms around each other's shoulders, bumping the sturdy table now and then. They good-naturedly swore at each other. The men knew not to make too much noise on night guard duty, but there had never been trouble with the Cherokee at Fort Cass. Guard duty was more a nightly ritual than a necessity, and they knew the officers wouldn't check on them. Mohe watched them from behind a thick oak tree for a few minutes and decided to enter the fort another way. As drunk as they were, they had rifles waiting at their feet.

The fort consisted of many buildings and covered miles of ground. The General's Headquarters, living and sleeping quarters, the general store, gardens, kitchens, and many other buildings made up what seemed like a small town. With two thousand soldiers there already and five thousand more to come to remove the Cherokee people from their homes, it was like a sea of men waiting. These men slept in long, one-story buildings ringing the inside courtyard. It would be easy for Mohe to climb in the small windows left open to get some air moving in the stuffy buildings.

The guarded front gates weren't the only way to get in. Mohe had been to the fort before with Waya for the unsuccessful negotiations to stop the removal. He had seen the huge, open area loading docks at the rear of the main plaza where food supplies were delivered. There was no security at the docks. He walked quietly around the back of the fort and entered the main courtyard through a small door by the docks. He looked up and saw an enormous flag waving in the night sky, brushing against the stars. But the beauty of the flag soon turned into a symbol of terrible injustice. He crept silently to the nearest sleeping quarters, raised the slightly opened window, and stepped in without a sound.

As he stood in the dark, he heard snoring from all directions and smelled white men's sweat, nauseating him. It was warm inside with several hundred men giving off body heat. Soldiers lay sleeping, stacked in bunk beds. Once inside, he acted quickly. His war cry startled the first sleeping soldier he came upon. As he lifted his long Bowie knife high above his head, he paused. The soldier, now fully aware of what was happening, sat up suddenly, although it seemed the man was moving in slow motion to Mohe. The soldier had on a torn, gray undershirt and long underwear bottoms and looked oddly vulnerable. As the soldier reached toward him, Mohe slashed the man's arm out of instinct to protect himself.

In that second, Mohe realized killing an innocent man was not revenge but murder. He dropped the knife and raised both hands over his head. Soldiers who had been sleeping only seconds before sprang into action, knocking Mohe down. There was a great deal of shouting, and everyone was awake. A short, muscular soldier sprinted to the horse corral and grabbed a rope.

Three men pulled him to his feet and tied him up, tightening the thick, coarse rope around his arms and shoulders. Two men dragged him, stumbling through the barracks, into the central plaza, and then to the holding cell in the fort's jail area. They untied him and pushed him to the ground. The sound of the gated metal door slamming shut echoed throughout the plaza.

At first, Mohe whimpered to himself. What had he done? Then, he spoke to the spirits of his ancestors, asking for strength. He did his best to rest on the cold earth that night because he knew that sunrise would bring both honor and grief.

Callie awakened early the next morning, rested and settled. As she stretched, she again felt a rush of pride for having talked Mohe out of his dangerous plan. She put on her mother's necklace and patted it against her chest. A long, orange beaded rope hung from her slender neck, and at the bottom of the beads was a round, flat disc, two inches in diameter. The disc had ten rings of orange and red beads along the edge, and yellow rays shot out from the center. It looked as if the sun was waking up. Callie put it on every morning to remind her of her mother's love. Each evening, she set it back in its special blue clay bowl that she and Ama had dyed with blueberry juice after Dove was gone.

Callie loved Rattlesnake Springs, snuggled into the rolling hills. Each of the thirteen settlements that made up her village had a central plaza and horse corrals tended by young warriors like Mohe. Most of the thirteen thousand people who lived there were farmers and sold their extra corn and other food to the fort cooks. Callie knew her people and the soldiers were equally fond of fresh rabbit, squirrel, raccoon, and deer. Her favorite was turkey.

The round log homes usually had three rooms, two sleeping areas, and a central room for cooking and resting. Deer, buffalo, or bearskins covered the ground, and Callie's hut smelled like Ama's bread and Waya's pipe. The village homes were arranged in a semi-circle, and people knew and cared for their neighbors that way. Noisy children and cackling chickens ran free everywhere. Callie especially loved that their home was always ready for people to stop by. Her grandmother's friendly nature practically invited neighbors to come in.

Callie lived with Ama, "the water of life," Waya, "the wolf," and Little Wolf. Ama seemed to know everyone and everything. Her long deerskin dress, fringed at the bottom, and her yellow beaded necklace made her look fun and happy. Before she was born, Callie's father had gone hunting and never returned, and after her mother had died five years earlier giving birth to Little Wolf, she and her brother moved into their grandmother and uncle's hut. Every day she missed her mother and remembered many times when Dove took out their braids, and they danced together. Callie thought even her mother's lovely hair danced.

Eager to begin her day with the Cherokee morning song, she jostled her brother awake. Little Wolf fussed, whined, and would not budge. With one eye closed, he peaked out at her from under his warm bearskin blanket. But when she told him that their grandmother had cornbread waiting, he jumped out of bed. He and Callie wrapped wool blankets around themselves, stepped outside, faced east, and chanted:

> *We thank the sun for his rays.*
> *We are grateful for all life.*
> *We are only guests on this earth.*
> *We will treat all with love. W'en de ya ho.*

"Are we done? I have to pee—now!" Without waiting for an answer, Little Wolf's short, fast-moving legs carried him into the wooded area near their hut, about one hundred yards away. Both his and Callie's legs, like all Cherokee children's, had small burn scars from sitting too close to fires that shot out hot ashes. She soaked in the early morning sunlight as it peeked through the tall, thick tree canopies. Little Wolf sprinted back to Callie's side when he was done, because even though the woods were beautiful, they were also a little threatening. She tossed him on her back for a ride.

Callie's memory of Waya's muscular shoulders carrying her and Little Wolf always made her smile. Her uncle usually wore deer-leather leggings and a tan cotton shirt. He had multiple ear piercings with small, gold hoops dangling from his ears, and, at times, a red-and-white striped cloth turban covered his black hair. When Callie watched his hoops sway as he moved, she thought he looked strong and elegant at the same time. He spoke and wrote English, but only because it was necessary to communicate with the government soldiers at the fort.

"Let's go to the fields. The wild turkeys have been digging up the beans again," Ama sighed as she walked out the door. They had harvested the corn a month ago but there were still a few bean plants left. Callie's favorite, the summer squash, looked plump and ready to eat. The beans, corn, and squash were called "sisters", taking care of each other and encouraging growth.

"We'll be right there, Ama," Callie called out as she stuffed another piece of cornbread into her mouth.

"Do we have to? I don't want to work. Uncle made me a new toy top, and I want to spin it around and around today!" Little Wolf said.

"I like your toy, too. You can take it to the fields." And with that, Callie firmly took his hand and hurried to catch up with Ama. On the way out, Little Wolf grabbed his white beechwood top, painted with blueberry juice stripes. He gripped it tightly in his small, brown fingers. Callie thought it looked like he was afraid one of those wild turkeys might steal it away.

"Hi, Lula!" Callie called out as Lula popped her head out of her door. Another small head peeked out. Callie smiled when she saw Blossom pointing to Little Wolf's blue toy.

"We're going to the fields now, and the traders are coming later this morning. Let's play in the afternoon."

Lula waved, but as Little Wolf and his toy walked out of Blossom's line of sight she cried. Lula picked her up, gave her a kiss on the cheek and sang her a silly song. They disappeared inside their door, but Callie heard Blossom's giggles float through the morning air.

When Callie and her brother arrived at the field, Ama and Waya were talking in hushed tones. They were in Ama's herb garden, considered the finest in all of Rattlesnake Springs. Callie was proud that Ama had a special way with plants and herbs and combined them to make many kinds of medicine for people. Ama spoke often about the goodness of the earth. Callie thought her grandmother was pretty with her long, gray braids smoothed out with bear grease, and deep wrinkles around her eyes, well earned from years of smiling. Callie's curiosity about what they were discussing led her to do some weeding closer to them. She caught most of the conversation.

"I feel the *U-ya* everywhere. The evil spirit has come to our village, and he will not leave until his work is done. I know this, son," said Ama. Callie was surprised and frightened to hear her grandmother talk about the *U-ya*.

"I had another meeting with General Scott and again asked that the United States government leave us in peace. He refused and is determined to move us off this land. He said he's obeying his President Jackson and so must we," said Waya.

"Their law is not our law. Are we to be treated like animals, herded out of the way? Will they destroy our fields to plant their own? How would we get to the place they force us to go?

How and why does so much greed consume them?" she said.

"I wish I had answers. I will meet with the other tribal leaders today," he said. Callie waited, breathless, and after a long pause, he added more quietly, "When I offered the general the peace pipe, he turned his head away."

When she saw Ama's trembling hand grab her son's thick wrist, she sucked in air with a small gasp. Ama looked her way and then called out.

"Callie . . . Little Wolf, come here. Let's start our morning with the Bee Song!" she said.

Callie stood and smiled, but her legs were shaking, and she heard the tremor in Ama's voice. She wasn't sure what the conversation meant, but the U-ya was wicked and powerful. Little Wolf scrambled over to his grandmother, almost tripping on his deerskin leggings. Ama had sewn him a new pair, but they were too long for his short legs. He set his top down.

Callie began the Bee Song with a loud, buzzing noise, and Little Wolf jumped up and down in anticipation. In the poetic language of the Cherokee, everything sounded like a song, but this children's tune was especially sweet to Callie. It went like this:

> *"The bees might bite us, but they also make food for us.*
> *Their honey is the best. Thank you, Bees. Oh! Oh! Watch out!"*

The song ended in a game of tag as the "bee" chased the children. Callie often made sure Little Wolf escaped the naughty bee. But Ama didn't play like that when she was the bee.

She caught them both in a big hug and buzzed loudly in their ears until they all collapsed to the ground in laughter. Her warm, rough hands always made Callie feel safe.

Callie noticed Waya was watching from a distance as if he realized she had overheard his discussion with Ama. Now that she was fourteen, there were many things she could understand and wondered if Ama and Waya would tell her more about leaving their land if she asked. Her stomach tightened.

"Callie, I need your help with the squash. Come," he called.

She trotted to her uncle's side, and he playfully swiped at one of her long, thick braids.

"Ha! I don't need help, but I do need to use your horse tail to keep the flies off me!" He swung at her braid again. He had lost two fingers on his left hand to a farming ax, but it always seemed to Callie that he had easily adjusted to having only eight fingers. She giggled and reached around his waist to give him a hug.

"I have good teeth like a horse, bad eyes and ears like an old dog. My life is happy, and I will live many more years. Worries have come to me, but most of those things I lost sleep over never happened." He went on, "I want you to understand how brave, intelligent and kind the Cherokee people are. I want you to know that we are stronger than the *U-ya*. Courage is within us, patiently waiting to help us, waiting to wake up. This is who your people are, and this is who you are."

Callie was quiet, looking directly and clearly into his eyes. She realized he knew she had overheard his and Ama's conversation. Suddenly, she grabbed her ponytail and began swatting it around his face. "Fly, fly!" she yelled.

Her uncle smiled. Callie understood that there was nothing more he would say to her about the removal, because there was nothing more he could say. There was no way to prepare for this. It was as if a disease was waiting in the woods, ready to sweep into the village unannounced. Even Ama, with her best herbs and medicine, couldn't stop it, and Callie knew it would be deadly.

– 4 –

Hideaway

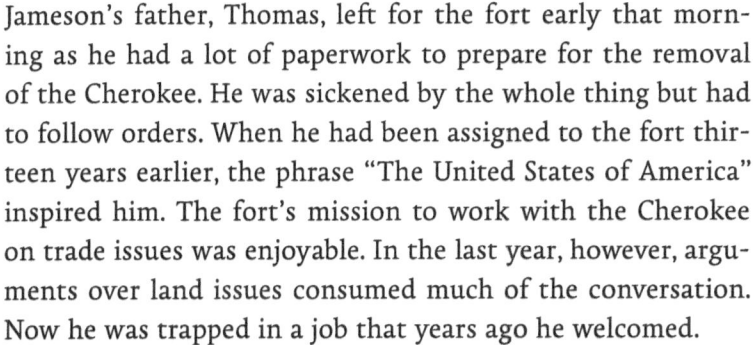

Jameson's father, Thomas, left for the fort early that morning as he had a lot of paperwork to prepare for the removal of the Cherokee. He was sickened by the whole thing but had to follow orders. When he had been assigned to the fort thirteen years earlier, the phrase "The United States of America" inspired him. The fort's mission to work with the Cherokee on trade issues was enjoyable. In the last year, however, arguments over land issues consumed much of the conversation. Now he was trapped in a job that years ago he welcomed.

He heard the soldiers talking about a Cherokee warrior who had been captured and was not surprised when a soldier told him the general wanted to meet with him. General Winfield Scott was the highest-ranking officer at the fort and Thomas was the second highest, so when he entered the general's quarters he saluted.

When he was told he could sit, Thomas straightened his uniform jacket before folding his powerfully built body into the small chair in front of the general's shiny cherry wood desk. A fire warmed the room with a floor-to-ceiling stone fireplace. With a smug look of satisfaction, a soldier pulled a young Cherokee warrior by a rope, with his hands tied together at the wrists, into the large office.

The general's small, beady eyes regarded the young man

suspiciously as his sizable body made his wooden chair creak. He always dressed in full, formal, blue military uniform with two rows of large, round, gold buttons running down from his neckline to the waist, and shoulders fringed with gold, rope-like curls hanging from them. His nickname was "Old Fuss and Feathers" among the more irreverent soldiers, referring to the extreme interest in his own appearance. Thomas was too professional to call him by his nickname even though he thought it suited him.

Thomas glanced at the frightened young man. His eyes were clear as he looked at them, but Thomas saw the sweat on his forehead and smudged war paint. The general gave Mohe permission to speak.

He began, "I came for revenge, sir. But now I come only for justice. The innocent do not deserve my anger. It is the man who stole my horse I look for."

The general had a strong-smelling cigar hanging from his lips. He took a long, slow inhale before laying it in a hollowed-out stone ashtray packed with ashes. After he exhaled, he said nothing, so Mohe continued.

"My name is Mohe. I met you when I came to a meeting with Waya a few months ago. A soldier stole my horse. I thought to steal my horse back, but this man is evil and would again take him from me. I chose instead to harm the first soldier I came upon last night, knowing I would not find the actual thief. But as I lifted my knife, I knew it was wrong to harm an innocent man. The soldier moved toward me, and I cut his arm. It is not a deep wound. I dropped my knife and surrendered."

Scott scowled at him. "That soldier you harmed is in the doctor's quarters getting his arm sewn up. I don't believe your apology. You're a threat and have done us harm. You will pay for this crime. Tomorrow at sunset, you'll hang."

Mohe's head fell forward. "This is not right, sir. I—" he said but was firmly interrupted.

"The United States government and I will decide what is right," said Scott. He pushed his chair back from his desk slightly. "How many times must I remind your people of the paternal caring and interest I have shown you? You and your leader, Waya, don't seem to understand that you must follow the laws of the United States. Your tribal laws mean nothing, and what I say is the law. Get him back to jail."

Thomas closed his eyes for a moment and tried to calm himself. Mohe was silent as the soldier who had brought him to the general grabbed the end of the rope binding his hands and yanked, causing him to fall to one knee on the wooden planked floor. He got up, regained his composure, and stood tall and proud. He looked directly at Scott, and the general lowered his eyes. The soldier pulled again, and they left the room.

"Our soldiers are not angels, Thomas. They can be impulsive, and taking a Cherokee horse is not something I am concerned about at the moment. I have to organize this damn removal. However, to have one of their kind kill or attempt to kill a man for a horse is unforgivable," said Scott. With his right hand, he fluffed up the gold cording on his left shoulder.

Thomas was shaken by the whole incident. Although not surprised at the general's order, he could not challenge him directly. Instead, he said, "I understand the severity of this Cherokee man's actions, sir. But I wonder at the wisdom of hanging him versus a lesser punishment. Everything will change soon. He is young and well respected in Rattlesnake Springs and has taken part in trade negotiations fairly and intelligently."

"Don't speak to me of the 'intelligence' of these savages. He will pay! And don't talk to anyone about this. The last thing I want is Waya finding out about it before it's done," said Scott.

Jameson was kicking a large stone around in his front yard when he saw his father walking slowly toward their small, white-shingled home; he knew something was wrong. Their home, like that of other officers including Geroge's father, William, was set outside the fort's ten-foot-high walls. Jameson and Katherine had joined Thomas at the fort when he was two years old. The family was well respected by the soldiers, and Katherine loved teaching school and didn't mind patching the holes that seemed ever-present in Jameson's pants.

His father paused when he reached Jameson and said, "Son, there will be a hanging tomorrow afternoon of a young Cherokee man who attacked a soldier over a stolen horse. I don't want you, George, or any other children to see this. You must not be here for it."

"Did the Cherokee man kill the soldier?" Jameson asked. This was unusual as the Cherokee were not generally threatening.

"He did not. I don't believe he deserves to die."

"Well, then tell that to General Scott. Stop this from happening, Pa."

"I talked to the general. He didn't listen."

Jameson felt his neck tighten and his stomach was unsettled. He stayed outside, quietly playing with a stick until lunch.

Jameson took his seat at the table, looking forward to the boiled potatoes, creamed chicken, and warm biscuits his mother had prepared. Splashes of color were everywhere in the small home, and sunlight poured in the south-facing windows. Katherine scooped out the delicious-smelling stew into heavy, cream-colored bowls.

"How did your meeting with the general go? I saw Mary and William at the general store early this morning, and he told me a Cherokee man attacked a soldier last night," Katherine said.

"I'm afraid it is true, Kathie. A young warrior attacked a soldier in revenge over a stolen horse. Scott says he will hang tomorrow at sunset. I know a few soldiers mean enough to steal a horse. I think it might have been John Payne. He's a rotten one. Anyway, I told Jameson to be nowhere near it."

Jameson looked down at his plate, but a shiver ran through him when he heard Payne's name.

"This can't be true! Our relationship with the Cherokee people is falling apart. Does no one have to pay attention to the legal treaties we made with them years ago?" said Kathrine.

"The treaties are losing power every day. And I seem to be losing my power too." Thomas took off his spectacles, set them on the table and rubbed his entire face with both hands. Jameson waited, and his father continued, "Things will go forward, and soon soldiers will round up the Cherokee and force them off their land. Farmers and settlers will take it over. There's no way to stop it."

"I can't believe it. I will not. I read in the *Chronicle* newspaper there is a group of women who are writing to Congress to stop this removal. I'll sign this petition." After a pause, she said, "We are abandoning the Cherokee, our own friends."

Jameson saw his father was tired and knew the hanging was heavy on his mind. His father had been less energetic than usual for a few months, but Jameson was distracted today, trying to eat lunch quickly and get out of the house. Katherine glanced at him, changed the mood at the table, and made small talk about the weather as they finished their meal.

"Jameson, have you enjoyed your morning off school? It's been a long week, and I'm glad to reward my students with the day off. I know reading isn't your favorite subject, but why don't you read some of this lovely adventure book right now?" She picked up a copy of *The Spy,* by James Fenimore Cooper that was lying by the kitchen cupboards. "I think you'll like it," his mother said in her most convincing tone.

"Maybe I'll get to that tonight, Ma. But now it's time to play with George." And he backed out the door into the late autumn sunlight.

"Let's play Jack Straws! Come on, let's go!" George's thick, gray cotton shirt was chronically dirty from playing, even after his mother had given it a good scrubbing. Jameson smiled when he saw that his friend had been waiting impatiently outside his house.

"Well, that sure was my plan," said Jameson.

The boys raced each other to their hideaway. Set in the woods, it was centered a half mile between Fort Cass and Rattlesnake Springs. The boys had spent the summer building their secret place. They hadn't told their parents or other kids at school about it. Jameson was surprised when George asked Callie to see it but had warmed up to the idea after the snake incident.

The hideaway was large enough for four people to stand in. The boys had arranged small, sturdy tree limbs, each about six feet tall, in a wide circle. They set them close together, and the sticks stood straight up, dug into the ground for support. There was a small door, made of limbs and twine, that opened and closed. The roof had more small limbs mixed in with leaves to protect it from the rain. They had bound the entire unit on the outside with thin, flexible branches. It was quite sturdy. A strong oak tree stood guard outside.

Inside were three tree stumps they used as chairs or tables. They had "borrowed" George's father's ax while he was at work to make them. George had taken some large, partially burned candles from his mother's general store that were in the pile of broken things she threw out every week. He also had grabbed two blankets that the moths had gotten to from her discard pile. The holes didn't bother him, and they were proud of all the furnishings. They had reserved one corner for game supplies.

George went to the game area and picked up thirty sticks for Jack Straws. He and Jameson had whittled them smooth with their small pocket knives. He walked outside and stacked them loosely to create a tower of foot-long sticks. Jameson went first, carefully pulling a random stick out from the tangled mess. George took his turn and pulled out another one. They kept taking turns, trying not to disturb the tower with one of their tugs. When Jameson's attempt tumbled the remaining sticks, George gave out a hoot.

"Yeah! I won! I'm pretty good at this game, ain't I? I knew just which one to pull out so as for you to lose!"

"Well, it looks to me like you just got lucky."

"Nope, nope. I did it right!"

"Hey, do you want to watch me hit a rock off this stump? Go find me a big branch that I can bat it with," said Jameson.

While George scurried around, Jameson put a stone, the size of a small ball, on top of a four-foot dead tree stump outside the hideaway. Jameson slowly walked around the setup, eyeing it as if it were the enemy. He decided that to do this best, he had to practice the correct angle in the air with the thick, sturdy branch George handed him. Jameson's mother had recently washed his shirt, and he hated that his clothes were always stiff after that. He worked at loosening up his arms, shaking them this way and that.

After a few minutes, George looked irritated. "Come on, hit it! What are you waiting for? That rock is just gonna fall off the stump from boredom."

Jameson ignored his friend, stared at the rock, got into position, and took a mighty swat. The branch broke in two and the rock flew into a grove of small trees twenty yards away. He was surprised at his own strength.

"Holy Moses! I ain't never seen you hit it that far! I can see your arm muscles through your shirt!" George exclaimed as he ran to retrieve the rock.

Jameson stood casually in place with slightly more weight placed on his right leg, thinking it made him look strong.

"Did you hurt your leg? You look like you're going to tip over," George said when he came back.

"Naw," said Jameson as he straightened up. Then he straightened up again to his full height.

Jameson heard a rustling in the brush, followed by a mangy dog plowing through the trees. He pounced on George, who smiled at him with obvious affection. George gave his dog a few pats on the head. King was a sight to behold. The dog had curly black and white fur and stood about two feet tall. His big, bushy tail seemed as if it would never stop wagging. He looked like a small, shaggy pony and was always picking up sticks and dropping them in front of people, hoping someone would play. But when George picked up a stick and threw it, King didn't catch on. He would run after the stick, pick it up, wag his head back and forth, playfully growling. Then he dropped the stick. The "bring the stick back to the person who threw it" part never took hold. Jameson had seen it many times and always laughed at George's frustration.

"Aw, ma sent King to get me. I took him here the other day, so he knows where the hideaway is, but I haven't told ma where we are. I'm keeping our secret! I've got to do my arithmetics—again. That's all I ever do, seems to me. You get to play as long as you want. I sure wish I was you."

Jameson thought for a minute and said, "Well, you don't want to be me. You want to be you. I'll help you with your arithmetics, though. Let's go."

As they walked home, Jameson asked, "Have you heard about the hangin' tomorrow? They are going to hang a Cherokee man from Rattlesnake Springs. I sure enough don't know the exactness of all of it, and pa says it wasn't good what he did, but he didn't do nothin' to get hung for."

George was unusually quiet for a moment. "Shucks, I didn't know about that. It feels like bad things seem to be happening lately."

"I agree with you there. Let's go to the hideaway tomorrow. I don't want to see that sad hangin'."

"Just what I was thinkin'," said George.

– 5 –

Traders

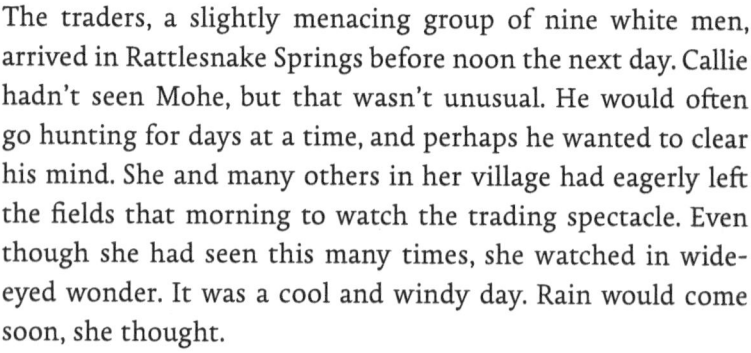

The traders, a slightly menacing group of nine white men, arrived in Rattlesnake Springs before noon the next day. Callie hadn't seen Mohe, but that wasn't unusual. He would often go hunting for days at a time, and perhaps he wanted to clear his mind. She and many others in her village had eagerly left the fields that morning to watch the trading spectacle. Even though she had seen this many times, she watched in wide-eyed wonder. It was a cool and windy day. Rain would come soon, she thought.

She saw three wooden, twenty-foot-long canoes, drifting slowly and carefully down the treacherous Hiawassee River. The river had many dangerous undertow currents that could draw a swimmer to his death in minutes. Callie knew the men were skilled canoeists, skilled in making money too. The canoes were full of items to exchange with the Cherokee in return for deer, beaver, and bear hides. The deer hides were especially valuable in Europe and were made into high-quality, soft gloves for wealthy women in London and Paris. Men favored beaver pelt hats. What little the traders paid the Cherokee was later tripled in profit when they loaded the goods onto the enormous ships heading for Europe.

The traders were dressed in every manner of fur and hides. Many wore raccoon skin hats, which usually included the animal's fluffy, black-ringed tail hanging down the back of its owner. Rifles lay at their sides in the sturdy canoes. The man in charge sat at the front of the largest canoe. He waved his hands in the air and shouted directions to his men as they were being pulled ashore by strong Cherokee men.

"Where is your leader?" the trader asked as he lightly stepped out of the canoe.

A warrior, bowing his head slightly, replied, "Waya is coming."

Callie was proud of how spectacular and regal her uncle looked as he passed through his people on the way to meet the traders at the shoreline. A red cape was slung around his tan cotton shirt. A striking half-moon shaped brass necklace, hanging on a thin strip of leather, graced his powerful chest. Waya had tied back his black hair and, on his head, woven into his hair, were several stunning, long bird feathers of blues and browns. At his side, in a fringed leather holster, hung his large hunting knife.

Callie and many other children sat, squirming, on the ground and, like the traders, waited impatiently. Other villagers stood in small groups, talking and laughing, also anxious for things to begin. Little Wolf wiggled at her side, wanting to get up and play with his top. "Soon the trading will start, and we need to be quiet. You can play later. For now, hold your top tight. That way, it won't run away!" Callie said, giving him a tickle.

People greeted Waya as he walked by, and he took time to talk with them. He saw Mohe's mother and asked, "Where is your son today? He could have helped me with these traders, not always honest men."

She smiled. "He told me he was going hunting for a few days but will be back soon. Good trading!"

Waya moved through the crowd and, finally, having been in no hurry, stopped at the bank of the river and faced the man who had been shouting orders when they arrived.

After greetings, the lean, tight-faced trader the others

called Isaac said, "How many skins do you have?" His raccoon skin hat dwarfed his head.

"We have two hundred and ten deer skins for you, fifty-two bearskins, decorated pipes, and pottery. What do you have for us?" Waya said. His voice carried through the crowd.

"We bring you shovels and other farming tools, cotton shirts, clothes, alcohol, and guns."

The traders took their wares out of the canoes and laid them on the short prairie grass in long, tidy rows. Waya motioned for seven warriors to bring out the skins lying behind his hut, and they also placed them neatly on the grass for inspection. Waya and his warriors, along with the nine traders, walked in and out of the rows, picking things up, turning them over, and calculating their value.

After one hour, they were ready to deal. Waya knew that some of his warriors wanted alcohol, but he had seen it destroy good men. He would take some alcohol but not much. He wanted clothes and hunting rifles. But mostly, Waya wanted the tools whites used that made farming easier. After the trading was done, Isaac and Waya exchanged a stiff goodbye, and the traders moved downstream to Fort Cass, not looking back.

Jameson awoke to the sound of the bugle player blasting out reveille, followed by a ceremonial gunshot that echoed through the river valley, just like he did every morning. But this morning, the fort was busier than usual in preparation for the traders his father mentioned would be there soon.

Two men raised the United States flag, and the soldiers began their day. After breakfast, the men tended to their duties. Some soldiers worked in the garden, others made sure the horses, chickens, and other animals, as well as the oxen who pulled the heavy supply wagons, were fed. They practiced marching drills, following orders shouted in short, sharp words. Some fished in the fertile Hiawassee River, and others played pool in the recreation room on the two wooden tables they had built. The Cherokee and military leaders sometimes used the recreation room for important discussions on trade and legal issues.

Much of the time the men were free to go about activities of their choosing after dinner, and at 11:00 p.m. the tall gates of the fort closed. If the soldiers stayed too long in the saloons in Charleston, they might end up sleeping on the ground that night outside the gates. The popular High Hopes Saloon featured a boisterous upright piano player pounding out lively, if out-of-tune, songs on weekends. But whiskey, cards and gambling were the real draw for most of the men, and the High Hopes Saloon was happy to supply those.

Jameson got dressed and walked to the fort but stayed on the fringes, watching the traders move to the central plaza where General Scott and Jameson's father were waiting for them. After grand handshakes, Scott led Thomas and Isaac, the head trader, to his office. The other traders and a few soldiers did some business in the plaza. Jameson overheard the traders bragging about how they had taken advantage of the Cherokee people. The banging of hammers caught his attention over the sound of the conversation. A couple of soldiers were busy building a small scaffold. He knew what it was for and was glad to be in his hideaway by the time it would be used to hang the Cherokee man.

General Scott, with a pompous and composed look, was interested in only one thing from Isaac. Guns. Because he was not part of the military, Isaac didn't address Scott as "sir." Even though the general knew this, every time Isaac spoke, Thomas saw the general's irritated frown.

"There's a hanging of a murderous Injun today at five o'clock, so I have little time. How many guns did you trade with them and what kind?"

After General Scott took a seat behind his massive desk,

Isaac and Thomas sat down. The general picked up a half-smoked cigar that had been resting in the stone ashtray and lit it. The room always smelled of cigar smoke. Thomas knew enough to not say much at these, or most, meetings. He adjusted his small, round, rimless glasses.

"Forty-two in total—twenty muskets and twenty-two rifles. Waya mostly wants farming tools," explained the trader.

"Did you sense any unrest?" asked Scott with a sense of hesitancy.

"No, why?"

"The United States government has asked Waya and his people to vacate the land they are on. For two years he has ignored us."

"I heard somethin' like that," said Isaac. He took off his coonskin hat and smoothed back his greasy, brown hair.

"Several thousand soldiers will arrive soon. We are preparing for them, adding cots and other things they will need. President Jackson has ordered us to move the Cherokee a thousand miles west."

"How in the hell will you do that? There are thousands of 'em!" Isaac laughed.

Thomas grimaced, wondering at the wisdom of telling traders this plan, but kept quiet. General Scott was interested in looking important, and sometimes that loosened his tongue too much.

"When the time is right, we'll attack at dusk, take their guns, and force them out of the village with the clothes on their backs, taking little else. They will walk, but we have some wagons for the elderly and young children. We don't wish for them to die, but this is a large group of Cherokee that need to be removed. Their leader is stubborn. Other villages, as you know, have already been vacated. I understand that many died of disease on the trail and in the holding camps we built along the way so they could rest and eat. That can't be helped. We have been quite generous, and of course, we accept these losses of life in return for the land."

"Does Waya know when this will happen?" asked Isaac.

"No. But, he'll know soon enough."

After the traders left that afternoon, pockets heavier, Jameson realized the time for the hanging must be close. George was sick, so Jameson planned on going to the hideaway alone, but first, he wanted to ask his father more about the removal. He was getting nervous thinking about what might happen to Callie. When his father didn't come home that afternoon, Jameson crossed the main plaza of the fort looking for him. He could hear and see most things that were going on.

The soldiers were preparing for the hanging. Many, but not all, soldiers believed the Cherokee were "savages," less civilized than white people. Their skin was darker, their language was not understandable, and most importantly, they had land white farmers and settlers "deserved." The soldiers thought it was fair the Cherokee people should be "removed," and they were prepared to follow orders.

As Mohe stood on the scaffold, the fort preacher asked the teenager if he wanted to say anything. A murmur went through the crowd of soldiers who had gathered as if they were surprised at this respectful gesture. A tired-looking soldier with a bandaged upper arm stood in the front row, staring up at Mohe. Jameson recognized John Payne, a slight smile curled on his lips, standing in the back.

The Cherokee man said in a loud voice, "Our people have worked to be your friends. We have tried to follow your laws. We learn your language and your religion. We trade with you. We feed you with our own crops. We hunt for you. But you steal from us. You cheat us. You harm us. There is no justice from the man who talks in two ways."

General Scott addressed Mohe in a booming voice from

the platform. "May God look upon you lightly, because the United States Army does not."

Jameson ran out of the plaza toward the hideaway, breathing hard.

– 6 –

Bones

Callie watched as Waya silently prepared for the important meeting with the general. He tied a red-and-golden striped scarf around his head instead of wearing what he knew was more threatening to the whites, a full-feathered formal headpiece. He wore an undyed cotton shirt, familiar to white people but added a deep red sash tied around his waist. A light blue coat, made for him by Ama, lay draped over his broad shoulders. Deerskin leggings and moccasins completed his ceremonial dress. At his side hung a large, leather pouch with fringes, slung across his shoulder. It usually carried a Bowie knife, but today, it was home to the peace pipe.

Callie knew that offering tobacco to an enemy was a sacred act and had the power to end wars. She'd never been allowed to touch the pipe but knew that it rested in a special red, woven reed basket along with the tobacco. A long handle made of hollowed-out deer antler made the pipe quite beautiful. Waya had formed the smoking bowl from wet clay found on the banks of the Hiawassee River and then baked it over a fire. The last thing he did was tie three eagle feathers onto the handle of the pipe with a strip of leather. Callie had often stopped Little Wolf from playing with it.

Before he left, Ama gave him advice. "Tell the general this: We have been on this land forever. People and animals lived happily on our earth island until it became overcrowded. Grandma Turtle succeeded in going to the bottom of the ocean to get mud to make the island larger but died because of her efforts. Now, out of respect for her, we call the world Turtle Island. We can all live together here," said Ama, who was making cornbread with Callie. She was surprised they were talking openly in front of her about this, and it frightened her. She focused on the bread.

"I don't think he will care about the story. He has different beliefs," Waya said.

Ama reached for a pinch of salt. "What can be so different? The creator, whatever you call it, wants us to live in harmony. The plants, animals, and people all share the same earth. None of us 'own' it, but we have taken good care of this earth. Why must we leave? What have we done wrong?"

Waya answered, "The whites believe individuals can 'own' the land. They want us gone so they can use the earth we are standing on now for their own homes and fields. They will grow wealthy, but the land will be stripped of its goodness. It will grow poor."

"The evil spirit *U-ya* is near. I don't know if you should be a powerful warrior with the general or ask for mercy, son."

Callie was frightened when he answered, "Neither do I."

Waya chose the best of his horses, a sleek caramel-colored stallion with small, white spots on his shoulders. He didn't enjoy going to the fort, and the dead earth without trees or birds in the central plaza always made him uneasy. The earth is the only thing that knows all of Cherokee history, and we must nourish it, he thought as he neared the gates. The white men are often ungrateful for all she gives people, and one day the earth will rebel. She would not be taken for granted any longer.

The soldiers standing guard at the gates were used to seeing Cherokee people come in and out for trade and other business and usually paid little attention to them. But once Waya had passed, both guards turned to stare at the regal man on his muscular horse prancing slowly through the plaza toward General Scott's quarters.

Housed in a large, red-brick, two-story building, it included a front patio complete with comfortable wicker rocking chairs. The soldier who had accompanied Waya into Scott's large office saluted, turned in a tight half circle, and walked out. General Scott sat down and lit a cigar.

"You may sit," said the colonel to Thomas and Waya.

"Thank you. *Wado*," Waya said in the white man's language and also in his own. He sat down on the uncomfortable, heavy wooden chair. He was used to sitting in smaller, lighter chairs, on benches, or on the ground.

General Scott took over. "This will be a short meeting. I have many things to do."

Although Scott was already taking control, Waya did his best to pace the conversation. He changed position in his chair. "General Scott, we have talked several times about this matter of removal."

"Yes, we have indeed been through this," Scott said and clenched his jaw.

Thomas saw Waya stiffen at the general's impatience, and he began again. He remembered Ama's advice. "This land has been ours since the beginning of time. The Creator put all of us here to live in peace. We are only guests on this earth. We believe—"

The general interrupted him. "Stop. I've heard enough. I met with you today because I thought I could finally convince you of how good I have been to your people over the past few years. But make no mistake. The United States military will take that land. I don't wish to harm your people, but how this removal proceeds is up to you. You can fight or you can understand that we are in charge. I suggest you do the latter."

Waya's heart wanted to plead, but his head knew he had to be rational. "General Scott, we have adopted many of your ways. There are many Christians among us now, and we have learned your style of farming. We sell our vegetables to you. Our children learn your language. Are we not friends?"

General Scott stood abruptly, but sat back down. He brushed at his gold shoulder ropes. After a pause, he said, "This is not about friendship. You are bound by the laws of the United States, and I will carry out those laws."

Waya spoke in a hushed voice, "Your laws are not our laws. We signed treaties. How can you move all of us? Rattlesnake Springs is a large village, and we are many thousands."

"We will prepare several hundred wagons for the elderly, sick, and small children. Some of you may take your horses. Beyond that, you will walk. This meeting has ended."

Thomas, who had remained tight-lipped throughout, stood as did Waya. He carefully pulled out the peace pipe and turned toward Thomas, offering him the pipe. Thomas's face softened. General Scott rose, glared at Thomas, and then at Waya.

"This meeting has ended, I said."

Waya carefully replaced the pipe in his shoulder bag, adjusted the sash around his waist, and turned to leave.

"There is one more thing," the general said. Thomas flinched. "One of your warriors, Mohe, I think was his name, was hanged yesterday. He tried to kill one of my men in revenge for a horse a soldier took from him."

Thomas saw Waya's face tighten, and shake his head slightly as if he hadn't heard correctly.

After a long puff on his cigar, Scott continued. "He said he knew it was wrong, and, thankfully, the soldier is alive. But I had no choice. What was I to do? You'll find his body on a gunny sack by the side of the loading docks at the back of the plaza."

Waya took a step back. His world had unexpectedly shifted, and his mind raced. Mohe's mother said he was hunting. What had happened? What had gone so wrong?

"Do the eyes of your Christian God see all that you are doing, General Scott?" said Waya before he abruptly walked out.

Waya's legs had turned to jelly and couldn't hold him much longer. He needed to sit on the closest log bench he could find. He found one along the walls of the sleeping quarters, not far from where Mohe had entered through the small window. Mohe did not go hunting. The general had carried out the hanging quickly so that Waya didn't intervene. General Scott had been careful not to let him know anything until it was done. Wave after wave of realizations washed over him.

The strong tribal leader could not sit nor show weakness, however. There were twenty or thirty soldiers milling around in the plaza, staring at him as he walked slowly out the front gates and around to the back of the fort. The smell of their fear and anger filled his head. He walked purposefully, step by step until he arrived at the loading docks. The soldiers, who had been unloading bags of potatoes from a wagon, stopped their loud banter when they noticed a man with a red-and-gold turban swirled around his black hair.

Waya immediately saw Mohe, a still form under three empty gunny sacks that had formerly held wheat. He sat on the ground next to his friend. The soldiers ignored him and went about their business, although they shared whispers and knowing looks now and then.

After ten minutes, he picked up Mohe and laid him over his powerful shoulder. Mohe was heavy and soft, as if overnight his body had both gained weight and lost muscle tone. Waya rebalanced himself and his load and walked back through the door into the plaza. Even though he could have avoided it and left the fort via the loading docks, he wanted the soldiers to see him and to see Mohe.

The soldiers did see them. There were several hundred men in the plaza now who parted as Waya moved through them as if they didn't exist. Thomas was among the men, and in his mind only, as it was too dangerous to follow through with it, he saluted both men.

Waya draped Mohe's body over his horse's back behind the saddle, got on, and exited the large entrance gate. On the mile ride back to Rattlesnake Springs, his head and heart were preoccupied with how to tell Mohe's mother.

Callie wasn't sure how long the meeting would last but stayed near the road to see her uncle's expression when he returned, hoping for a smile. From a distance, she saw him walking his horse slowly with something on the horse's back. As he got closer, Callie realized it was a body. Upon nearing the village, a small child saw them, stopped in her tracks, and ran home calling to her mother. Men and women came out of their homes as he walked his horse into the central plaza and gently placed the body on the ground. Only then did she recognize the face of her friend Mohe. Callie's wails added to the wails of the others as they saw his lifeless body.

The crowd made room for Mohe's mother who looked like she was fighting with the air to move forward. She looked down at her son and then stared at Waya in shock. The crowd was now eerily quiet. Ama moved toward her and held her hand. Callie stayed on the outskirts of the crowd, a lump growing in her throat, breathing fast.

Waya began. "Mohe, our brother, was hanged on the orders of General Scott last evening. His horse was stolen by a soldier, and in revenge, as is our tradition, he went to the fort. But he killed no one, realizing he couldn't find the guilty man, and that it was wrong to kill an innocent. Even so, he was hanged."

Mohe's mother whimpered to Waya, "No! This is not true! He told me he was going hunting for a few days. This cannot be true. Please, please!" Her voice rose, and she pulled at her deerskin dress.

Ama put her arms around Mohe's mother and held her while she sobbed. Waya continued, "I did not know of this until this morning. We pray to the spirits the last thing Mohe saw was the beautiful sunset."

Murmurs rippled through the crowd, and the sounds of the people returned, only louder and angrier than before. The men shouted warrior cries, and the women wailed in pain.

"There is nothing to be done at this time. The tribal council will meet tonight," he said as he picked up Mohe's limp body. Sadness like she'd never felt before crashed over Callie as she watched Waya walk side by side with Mohe's mother to the outskirts of town. The sky darkened as they were followed by large, black, noisy crows that seemed to come out of nowhere.

The remainder of the day was devoted to the elaborate ceremony at the large burial mound that housed the remains of the Rattlesnake Springs dead. A hole was dug in the mound and Mohe's body was tenderly laid inside, along with five intricately decorated arrowheads. There would usually be many days of mourning, many hours of comforting his mother.

The council met that night and with her house so near to the council house, Callie listened to her uncle's strong voice explain how the soldiers would force them to leave their homes and how General Scott would not listen to reason. Waya invited tribal members to speak, and he heard his people's anguish and righteous anger. He listened and listened throughout the night. He closed the meeting late when the moon hung high in the sky, saying the incident would be taken up again, although he knew it would not. He walked home and crawled under his bearskin blanket, trying not to wake his family. The mighty warrior breathed in hard and finally released his tears.

Callie lay under her bearskin blanket, wide awake and trembling, listening to her uncle softly cry. She'd never heard him do this and was afraid. When she finally fell asleep, she dreamed that the earth was growing bones.

Callie and Waya woke earlier than the others, and she asked him to step outside. It was time to tell her uncle the truth about how she knew what Mohe had planned to do. She began to weep. "I tried to stop him! I did! I saw the man steal Big Dog, but Mohe told me to not tell anyone. He wanted revenge. I thought I had talked him out of it, so I told him I wouldn't tell you. I thought he had agreed to not go to the fort, but I was wrong, so wrong. Oh, this is my fault. I should have told you, and you could have stopped him. Oh, please forgive me Uncle."

He held her as she shook with sobs. After a long pause, he gently moved her back and said, "I see your pain. You are right that it would have been best if you had told me what happened and what he said to you. You are too young to handle this kind of information. Mohe was torn up inside."

"I'm sorry. Mohe was angry, so angry at that man. But I truly thought he would not go to the fort. Did my words mean nothing to him?"

"All of our words are important. You did what you could to stop him. You must tell me these things, but Mohe made his own choice."

"But his choice ended in a cruel and unfair death! Aren't you angry?" Tears poured from her eyes. She pulled at her braids and realized the birds were singing. How could they be so happy when the world was falling apart, she thought.

"It was an unjust death. Mohe killed no one. For this, there is no answer, no justice. Even I could not have changed his mind. We cannot stop everything, but we must try. We must act."

"Can you stop the soldiers who want to make us leave our village? Can you?" She moved closer to him.

Waya paused. "I have done all I can. I cannot know the future. We must ourselves be strong, and in doing that, we are strong for everyone, for our people. "

"There is a fight going on inside me, Uncle. I don't know how to be strong. I'm angry and sad," said Callie. Her tears had slowed, and she wiped her eyes.

"My grandfather told me this story when I was your age and was struggling too," Waya said quietly. "A young boy told his grandfather a terrible battle was going on inside of him, a battle between two wolves. The boy said one wolf is evil: angry, hurtful, and has self-doubt. The other wolf is good: peaceful, hopeful, and believes in people's decency. The grandson asked his grandfather, 'Which wolf will win?' The old chief answered, 'The one you feed.'"

Callie closed her eyes. It was a fine story but regret and turmoil filled her heart. She was starving the good wolf.

– 7 –

Games

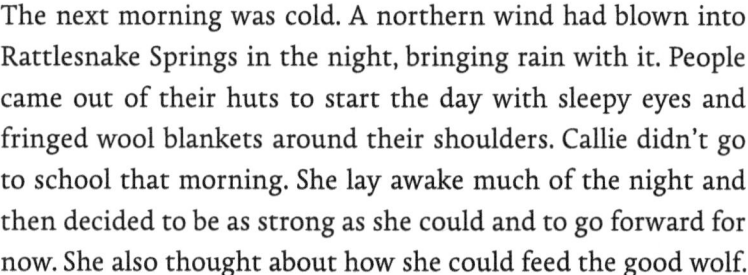

The next morning was cold. A northern wind had blown into Rattlesnake Springs in the night, bringing rain with it. People came out of their huts to start the day with sleepy eyes and fringed wool blankets around their shoulders. Callie didn't go to school that morning. She lay awake much of the night and then decided to be as strong as she could and to go forward for now. She also thought about how she could feed the good wolf.

At eleven o'clock, she walked to school and arrived right before Katherine rang the lunch bell. She had a red blanket wrapped tightly around her, covering her deerskin, shin-length dress. Her moccasins with festive red beadwork peeked out from under the long blanket.

As the rambunctious students poured out of the white, one-room schoolhouse into the yard, Callie stood to the side of the door. Some children said hello to her as they ran by, but when George and Jameson saw her, they stopped.

"Callie, what are you doing here?" asked George. "You weren't in school this morning."

"I make Mrs. Miller bread this morning," she said. Ama had helped her bake the bread and then rolled it in bear grease for flavor. As they baked together, her grandmother told her that one way to strengthen the good wolf in her was to do good things for others. She knew Ama was deeply sad, but she carried on.

"Can I have some?" asked Jameson.

Callie said, "May-be," smiled, and broke off a chunk of warm cornbread for Jameson and another for George. They stuffed it into their mouths. Before running off to play, George said, "Thanks! See you after school at the—" Jameson nudged and interrupted him before he let out the secret.

"Are you gonna tell the whole gosh darn school about our hideaway?" whispered Jameson.

Katherine saw Callie standing by the side of the door. "Hello! It's good to see you. What do you have in that pretty basket?" asked Katherine.

Callie took out the fragrant, round loaf of cornbread, minus a few chunks, and offered it to her. "I make bread for you, Mrs. Miller." Would she ever make bread for her teacher again, she wondered.

"My goodness! What a lovely surprise. Would you like to come into the schoolhouse until lunchtime is over? You can join us this afternoon too. We'll do some mathematics."

"I don't so much like sums," Callie said.

They walked into the schoolhouse, warmed by the black potbellied stove and its crackling cargo. Callie draped her blanket over a desk and took a seat. Katherine went to her own desk at the front of the room and got a piece of paper and something from a drawer. Callie watched her closely. Katherine took a seat at the student desk next to her, put the paper on Callie's desk, and motioned to put the bread on the paper. She held up a small glass jar.

"What is this?" Callie asked, tipping her head to one side.

Katherine untied a small piece of string that held on a cover made of red plaid cloth. As she took it off, the heavenly smell from the jam floated into the air.

"You made the bread, and I made strawberry jam a while

ago. Let's put them together and see what we think," said Katherine.

Callie watched carefully as Katherine used a butter knife to slather rich berry jam onto the cornbread. The Cherokee ate cornbread plain, and although Callie had tasted something like jam, this had much more sugar.

Her eyes widened with the first bite. She looked at Katherine, smiling. "I hear George say 'Holy Moses!' And I say it for this jam thing. More, please."

After eating half the loaf of bread with loads of fruity jam, Callie decided she needed to say what she had actually come to school for.

"Mrs. Miller, do you know about the hanging?" Her hands were slightly shaking.

Katherine's expression changed from enjoyment to concern. "Yes. I do. That was a terrible thing."

"Mohe was my friend. A bad man took his horse called Shiko Waka, or in English it is Big Dog. He was going to kill a soldier but didn't. Now he is dead," said Callie. Her head felt heavy as if she couldn't hold it upright.

"I'm sorry," Katherine said.

"I . . . I want the soldiers to know that Mohe was a good person. He was young. He told stories to the children in the village. He played with my little brother. If he had food, he shared it. If I was cold, he would wrap his blanket around me." Tears rolled down her cheeks, some falling onto her long braids.

Katherine said, "You want me to know that he was a good young man. I will tell my husband," said Katherine, looking closely at Callie.

"I tried to stop him. I didn't tell Waya because I thought I had stopped him. But I didn't." Callie felt as if she couldn't breathe and stood, trying to get more air into her lungs.

Katherine went to her and gently wiped her tears away with the white apron. Callie's breath softened with each sweet swipe of Katherine's apron. She moved closer to Katherine to make it easier for her to release the pain.

"Oh, dearest Callie. I see how sad you are. Maybe you think you could have stopped your friend. But it's not true. Mohe made his own decision. Perhaps it was wrong to us but right to him. What we can do now is remember all the good things about him you came to tell me about. We can remember him."

Callie's brown eyes began to dry and clear. As Katherine reached out and wrapped her warm arms around her, Callie thought of her mother. She thought about how Dove was friends with this white woman and how unusual, but good, that was.

She let herself melt into Katherine's arms. She forgave Mohe. She forgave herself. Finally, Callie could start to let him go, because she knew that for the rest of her life she would hold all of him close to her, all of who he was, all the memories in her heart.

After school, Callie went to play at the hideaway with George and Jameson. On the way there, she thought that George had probably ran and jumped the whole way. As she passed the river, she noticed it was wilder than usual with the stiff north wind stirring it up. Cautious but curious, she stepped inside through the small door of the hideaway. She wanted to lighten her spirit. The removal still hadn't happened. Maybe things could change. Maybe it can be stopped, she hoped.

The hideaway somehow resembled the huts of her village. The ground inside had been cleared of weeds and brush, and the boys had flattened the earth by walking on it repeatedly. She could easily stand and smiled at the three tree stump chairs and the used candles George had snuck out of his mother's store.

On the ground, she saw a small pile of rocks. "What is this?" she asked George.

"It's for a game called Marbles. M-A-R-B-L-E-S. Can you say it?" asked George.

"Ma-bells," she said and nodded her head.

Jameson let out a little laugh but immediately stopped when Callie glanced his way. George nodded enthusiastically to Callie. George crouched down on the ground and motioned for Callie to do the same. She did, and he placed ten small stones inside a large circle with edges that had been dug an inch deep into the dirt floor with Jameson's small knife. George showed Callie how to use her thumb and first finger to flick a large, round stone called the shooter. Taking turns, the goal was to knock out the small stones with the shooter, and whoever knocked out the most stones won. She immediately got the hang of it and was intent on building her little pile of stones. It was like a game called "basket dice" that she played kneeling on the ground with both girls and boys in her village.

She had not paid attention to Jameson during the marbles game, but Jameson had been watching her skillful playing.

"Gosh darn, I've been beat by a girl, Jameson! You try."

Jameson knelt and put the ten little stones back inside the circle. Callie realized they were going to play again and got into position two feet away from Jameson. Jameson shook his head slightly to focus. He eyed the stones and made imaginary lines with his fingers and a flourish to get his aim exactly right. He made quite a ceremony of it before letting the shooter fly. Callie watched in silence, thinking all this hand-waving and eye-to-the-ground strategy was unnecessary. However, Jameson was good, and he won the game by one stone.

"Why?" she asked as she mimicked his fingers measuring in the air.

"Because that's how you win; be the best. I like to win," said Jameson.

"Yes, he sure does!" hooted George.

Callie was now more comfortable and saw a sturdy stick

about a foot long and four inches in diameter in the corner. Lying around the stick were four coarse pieces of rope, and each had been tied to form a circle. She grabbed one of the rope pieces, and before the boys could stop her, she had untied it. With a mischievous grin, she laughed. This was easy for her as she and other Cherokee children were familiar with ropes and knots often used to tie up horses. The boys also laughed, and Jameson picked up the rope and retied it.

"No, Callie. This is for the game of Graces," said Jameson, still glowing from his win.

"How do we play?" asked Callie.

"Well," said Jameson. "There are different ways to play it, but this here is how we do it."

George picked up the thick stick, and Jameson, a bit grandly and methodically, picked up the four rings. They went outside into the cool October air, and George and Jameson stood fifteen feet apart. While George held the large stick firmly in front of him, Jameson carefully tossed, one by one, his four rings, trying to get them onto the stick. He got three of them on and, with a serious but pleased look, turned to Callie.

"It's your turn," he said and handed her the four rings.

George was nearly jumping up and down with excitement to see how Callie would do. She looked at George sternly, and he settled down and held the stick still.

"One, two, three, four," she counted as she quickly sent each rope ring to its home on the stick. Counting was one of the first things she had practiced when first learning English, and she loved the sound of the short, tight words.

She stood with her hands on her hips, grinning. Cherokee men played a ball-and-bat game called Anetso. Even though girls weren't allowed to play it at formal ceremonies, they played some version of it for fun. Throwing things accurately was one of Callie's strengths.

"She is better than you are at Graces!" said George. But when he saw Jameson's disapproving look, he continued. "But you're awful good. Yes, siree. Now that I think of it, she probably just got lucky," said George as his voice went from excited to squeaky.

"Callie win, win, win!" she sang, as she did a little dance and kicked her right foot behind her several times, turning in a tight circle, red moccasin beads dancing with her.

"Yes. Yes, you did," said Jameson.

Callie suddenly heard barking. She looked at the boys and said, "What?"

George's scruffy dog bounded at them, wagging, not only his shaggy tail but his entire body. Although he had black-and-white, curly fur, he looked gray from all the dirt that had permanently settled into his coat. The friendly dog headed straight to George and looked up expectantly, waiting for his pat on the head.

"Ah, darn! Ma sent King out looking for me. Tonight is bath night. Dang it!" said George.

Jameson laughed, and Callie smiled. "What is 'bath'?" she asked.

George blushed and made a scrubbing motion on his upper arm, followed by a frown. Callie knew he wanted her to think that he was as independent as Jameson.

"Bath is in river," Callie said.

"No. Ma puts hot water that she boils on the stove inside a big tin tub. Then, I get into the water, and she tells me to soak for a good, long time. But that water gets cold fast, so I pretend I'm soaking when I'm actually out of the tub, standing in my towel."

Jameson laughed again, and Callie playfully scrubbed her upper arm. "No! No baths!"

King walked over to Callie and investigated the smell of her deerskin skirt. Callie liked dogs, but they weren't owned by an individual in her tribe. Many happy dogs ran around Rattlesnake Springs and were fed by the community. Callie saw that King was special to George by the way he smiled at his dog.

She hesitantly bent to pat him, a bit too roughly, on his head. He looked up at her and continued to sniff her dress and wag his tail.

"King! Leave her alone," said George.

"He has name?"

"Sure does. His name is K-ing," said Jameson.

Callie watched Jameson's mouth say the word and tried it. "K-ing-er," she said.

George looked at her seriously. "No, it's just K-ing."

Callie eyed George mischievously and said, "K-ing- er!"

Jameson chuckled, but Callie could see George was in a grim mood about the bath. "I'll see you tomorrow. Come on, King, let's go home." As he turned to leave, he looked back at Callie and shouted, "Let's go, Kinger!"

As Jameson was putting the things neatly back into the game corner, he was taking in his unexpected loss to Callie. He wanted to ignore it, downplay it, or make excuses for himself. Maybe his wrist wasn't at its best today. He'd had to unload many heavy bags of supplies for Mary at the store the other day. Yes, that was it. His wrist had gone weak from all that lifting. But something tugged at him. Callie had won. She was better at this game than he was. Sometimes, things are just what they are, he thought.

The sun was setting fast, and he was hungry. His home was a fifteen-minute walk west of the hideaway, and Callie lived a fifteen-minute walk east. Jameson had never seen any of the homes in the Cherokee village and had thought little about them until now.

He gathered his courage and said, "I can walk you home. I mean . . . if you want. I mean, I know you can go by yourself, but I can go that way, too. Well—"

Callie interrupted him. "May-be. Yes."

She walked at a lively pace, and Jameson started off a little behind her, surprised at his luck. They walked a short distance through scrubby prairie grass and came upon a more worn-down path that Jameson hadn't ever noticed. He realized this was a kind of road used by the Cherokee people between their village and the fort. But the soldiers did not use this path to go to Rattlesnake Springs. They didn't go there at all. Now Jameson was going there.

"I've never seen this path," he said, but didn't know what to say next. He wanted to ask her about the removal. Would she have to leave? He wanted to tell her how horrible his government was. But he decided not to say anything because they were having such a nice day.

Callie had become quiet and seemed to have lost her good mood.

"Are your parents at your house?" Jameson asked, trying to get a sense of what to expect.

"No parents," she said.

Again, Jameson wasn't sure where to go in the conversation. "Oh," was all he could think of saying.

"My mother . . . she died."

"I'm sorry," said Jameson.

"But it is happy that she had my little brother, Little Wolf. She died from that birth."

"How old is Little Wolf?" asked Jameson.

Jameson saw Callie brighten and she stopped for a second. "Five!" Jameson noticed her sparkling eyes and smiled. He didn't know whether to ask where her father was or leave the conversation alone.

"You already know ma is the teacher, but maybe you don't know that pa is a soldier. He's a good soldier. Some can be mean."

Callie looked straight ahead. "My father is gone. Maybe he

died in a fishing or hunting accident like Little Wolf's father. I never saw him. Now I live with Little Wolf, my Ama, and my Uncle Waya."

"Well, it must be hard to miss your parents. Who is Ama?"

Callie's face relaxed as she turned to look at him. "Grandmother!"

Jameson smiled, "I am glad you have your ama. I miss mine. We came to the fort when I was two and my 'ama' lives far away. I hardly ever see her, but we write letters sometimes."

Callie said she didn't understand writing letters and that she was a bit tired of speaking so much English. As they neared her village, she walked faster and got ahead of Jameson. Jameson held back, not sure how far to go. He was about to turn around and head home for dinner when he noticed a wild raspberry patch to his right. The birds had eaten most of the fruit, but he saw several plump, red raspberries. He picked three of them and called out to her. She turned around.

He held the berries behind his back. "I'm going home. Maybe I'll see you tomorrow. I was thinking to ask what your mother's name was?"

As she turned to face him, her eyes softened. "Her name was Woya. It means 'Dove.' This is her necklace." She gently touched it.

"That sure is a pretty necklace. Well, see you," he said and awkwardly held out the slightly squashed raspberries to her.

His sudden movement surprised her, but she bent slightly to look closer at what he had in his hand. Her black hair shined in the setting sunlight, and he was mesmerized by it when her head popped up.

"Thank you! You are a nice friend." She took the raspberries and he heard her sing out the name "Woya, Woya" as she ran home.

– 8 –

Idea

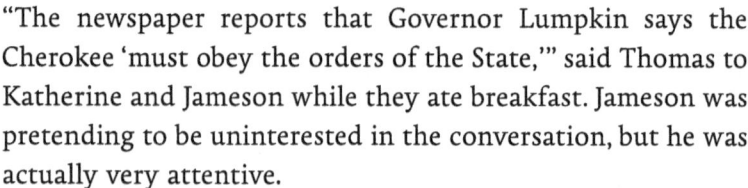

"The newspaper reports that Governor Lumpkin says the Cherokee 'must obey the orders of the State,'" said Thomas to Katherine and Jameson while they ate breakfast. Jameson was pretending to be uninterested in the conversation, but he was actually very attentive.

"But it was their state before it was 'our' state! Our Cherokee friends are suffering in other ways, too. Mary heard there was a Cherokee family who disagreed with each other last week about removal. The husband wanted to go, but his wife, Pearlie, such a pretty name, wanted to stay. They had a terrible argument! We're ripping their culture apart!" said Katherine.

"It's a tragedy. The governor calls people who are against removal 'ignorant and uninformed.' Well, I beg to differ!" said Thomas. His voice quivered, and he laid his fork on the table as if he had lost his appetite. Jameson was surprised at his father's strong emotion, usually well-controlled.

"Be careful with your words, dear. Will you have to be involved? Will you have to push these innocent people from their homeland?" Katherine asked.

"I'll try not to take part in the actual removal and will tell the general I need to stay back and in command of the fort. Even so, I feel as if I am contributing to this wrong."

Thomas paused. "It can't be stopped. Thousands of extra soldiers are already here and more come every day." He turned to Jameson, who had been quietly eating. "I understand you helped Mary unload supplies at the general store the other day. Thank you, son," said Thomas.

Jameson sat, stiff, in his usual simple, wooden chair at the small kitchen table. Was he helping the soldiers, too, by unloading their supplies, he wondered. That was the last thing he wanted. What would happen to Callie? What did it mean to "push" the Cherokee west? He wanted to ask more questions, but his parents were now deep in conversation.

He also did not want to reveal that he had been talking with Callie at the hideaway. He knew many people would not appreciate that he was playing games with a Cherokee girl, but at the same time he was angry at himself for thinking that playing Marbles and Graces with Callie was wrong. His parents didn't know about the hideaway, and he was anxious about the secrets that kept piling up in his life. He tapped the floor nervously with his right foot.

Jameson interrupted his father, but his words came out too loud. "Why can't you do something, Pa? You're the second-highest ranking officer in the whole fort! Are you just going to do nothing?"

Lately, he had been thinking that his father wasn't as strong as Jameson thought he was. What did it matter if his father was an officer in the military if he wouldn't or couldn't use his power? Which was it: wouldn't or couldn't? Did it matter? Jameson's shoulders slumped, and he put his fork down.

"Watch your tone. Speak to your father with respect," said Katherine.

"Son, I only have so much authority, and it's not enough to stop the United States government," said Thomas. He looked down at the table and let out a long exhale.

Jameson grew more agitated, and a picture of Callie formed in his head as he thought about her safety. It was as if his mother read his mind.

"I know you admire Callie, but it's best if you and she don't speak anymore. I don't think she'll be coming to school much longer. We have to think about what's best for her now," Katherine said.

Jameson sat without moving so that his head wouldn't explode from emotions so confusing that he couldn't put names to them. His father was weak, and his mother was controlling.

Jameson blurted out, "Why don't we and the rest of the white people go back to where we came from? We had land in the East. This is their land. I don't understand!"

His father sat still, looking as if he was lost in his own emotions.

Jameson hesitated. "Will the soldiers go to Callie's home?"

"Maybe, son." Then a moment later, he said, "Yes, they will."

Jameson stood and quickly left the kitchen. It didn't matter what his mother said. Callie was here, and he was going to be nice to her. He walked outside and kicked at rocks as hard as he could. He knew now what his emotion was. Its name was "rage."

Neither Jameson nor George could focus on school. Both boys were eager to go to the hideaway after Katherine rang the school bell three times before ending the day. Callie had been working in the fields all day with Ama and was also impatient to get to the hideaway.

"Ama, am I finished with my work?" she asked in her sing-song language.

As soon as Ama said, "Yes," Callie ran-skipped away for the afternoon. Ama was used to Callie and other village children running free, playing games and enjoying each other's company outside. The children would come home to eat or be offered food by neighbors and head right back out, often playing into the evening. Their laughter rang out everywhere in Rattlesnake Springs.

"Hello! I surprise you!" Callie said. She had hidden behind a bush and popped out at the boys when they arrived at the hideaway. She was tired of thinking about bad things.

"Holy Moses! You sure enough did surprise me," George said as he halted in his tracks.

Callie could see that Jameson was in a bleak mood by the way he only glanced at her as she walked inside. George went to the Marbles game circle and picked up his marbles, which lay scattered on the ground. They were made of clay from river-bank mud, rolled into balls, and left to dry in the sun until they were hard. Callie could see from the way he handled them that George was proud of his creation. She watched as he fumbled, trying to pick them all up. A few marbles fell out of his full hands.

"More surprise!" Callie said as she smiled at George. He looked at her and raised his eyebrows in anticipation. She pulled something out of the leather pouch that was always slung across her shoulder and handed it to him.

"This is for Ma–bels. I make it," she said.

George gently took the small basket from her outstretched hands. He turned the basket over and upside down to see every part. After the last time they played Marbles, Callie wove it from river cane and the thin branches of young white oak trees. She had smashed some of Ama's elderberries, mixed them with water, and let the basket soak in the rich purple-colored water. Finally, she set it in a sunny place to dry.

"Oh!" George said in an unusually hushed voice. "This is the nicest thing anyone has ever given me. Thank you." He sat down on the mud-packed ground and one by one laid his marbles in their new home.

Jameson watched it all in silence, but Callie noticed his

face starting to relax. "That's nice. Real nice of you."

"Do you want to play Jack Straws?" George asked as he carefully set the basket down. George and Jameson took the thirty smoothly whittled sticks out of the game corner and tossed them in a random pile outside in front of the hideaway.

"Show me," Callie said to Jameson.

Callie was the first to hear a horse's hooves coming toward them, plowing through the brush. John Payne pulled up hard on Big Dog's mouth bit, and she stopped.

"Well, mercy, mercy me! What do we have here?" Payne said as he glared down at them from the saddle. They met him with quiet stares.

"Here I am just mindin' my own business, takin' my new horse out for a little ride before I head into town for a whiskey—or four." He chuckled to himself and got off Big Dog, but held her tightly by the reins. George backed away from him, eyes wide.

"Why, I can see you boys have built yerselves a hiding place. Sure enough!" He walked Big Dog close to the open door, and when Jameson nervously stepped to the side for him, Payne looked inside. "You even got some chairs in here. Built it pretty sturdy, too, for two stupid boys."

The boys looked at each other. Callie knew what the word "stupid" meant and was about to protest when Payne turned his glare toward her. He looked at her for a moment before turning back to the boys.

"You know why you're stupid? Because you're playing with this Injun girl. What the hell is wrong with you?" he said and moved a step closer to the boys who were now standing side by side to the left of the open door. Callie, who stood to the right of the door, took a step closer to Payne and anger flared in her eyes.

She was also the first person to hear the barking and turned toward it. King bounded through the brush into the clearing and scooted to a halt, confused by the horse. He looked around and ran to George, but instead of jumping happily on him, the dog sat quietly at his side. Soon enough, however, he began barking again.

Big Dog moved back a few steps to get away from King, pulling on her reins. Payne stumbled. "Shut your dog up! Damn you! Shut him up!" he snarled at George.

Payne's tone surprised them, but before George could quiet his bushy-tailed friend, King moved toward Payne and snapped at his leg. Payne was quick to react and kicked King in his side. The dog flew backward five feet and lay there for a few seconds, whimpering. George ran to him, and the dog wobbled but stood up. He seemed more stunned than hurt. George knelt on the ground to pet him, and Callie walked over and patted King on the head. Jameson stood where he was, and Callie saw him clenching his fists. She didn't know what to do.

Payne got back on the anxious horse, who had been trying to back away from the chaotic scene. He thrust his long, sharp boot spurs into her sides, and she flinched and began to trot. He rode off without a word.

Callie was the first to go back into the hideaway. She went directly to one of the tree stump stools, sat down, and tried to quiet her quick breathing by putting her right hand over her heart. Jameson and George followed her in, taking their seats. Jameson wanted to ask her what she was thinking but didn't know how to say it. King limped in behind them and laid down at George's feet.

"That's . . . that's the man we saw before," said George, hands shaking as he pet King on his back, careful to stay away from the bruised side.

"He stole away Mohe's horse. That bad man is riding her, and Mohe is dead," said Callie, shock turning to anger.

"He's a rotten apple. That's for sure. How is King?" asked Jameson.

"I think he's alright. I don't know. What's wrong with that soldier?" said George.

"Maybe he's already drunk, even before he gets to the High Hopes Saloon. All the soldiers go there. There are a few taverns, but the soldiers like the High Hopes best. It's the biggest one in Charleston, and there's a piano player."

"How do you know these things?" asked Callie.

"Pa and I go to town sometimes after dinner to pick up things we can't get at Mary's store. We walk by there, and I can hear the piano and the soldiers. The more they drink, the louder they get."

"I want to go home," said George as he stood. King struggled to stand but then followed close behind.

"Goodbye. I am sorry about King-er," Callie said. George smiled back at her as they disappeared down the path.

"Well . . . well, I can walk you home again, if you want," Jameson said. He adjusted his suspenders.

"May-be. Yes," she said, as they both left the hut. Jameson saw her smooth out her braids and briefly touch her yellow-and-orange beaded necklace.

Jameson shook his head and grinned As she turned to smile at him, she tripped over a tree root hidden under the autumn leaves.

He was quick and grabbed her around the waist as she headed to the ground. Callie stood up and straightened her knee-length dress. "Thank you."

"Sure," he said as his voice cracked. He was often frustrated at his changing body but now was a little lightheaded and proud he had caught her. It surprised him how soft her deerskin dress was, and his cheeks suddenly seemed quite warm.

Callie kept walking but slowed to a stop. "You are strong. I am surprised." Jameson tried not to grin by focusing on a robin in a nearby tree.

As they neared her village, she said, "I want to go to the tavern where that bad man goes. I want to pet Shiko Waka. He is mean to her. She like apples. Take me to the place where he goes."

"What?" said Jameson.

"Take me to the place in town where that man goes. While he is inside, we will pet Big Dog and give her apples. We go tomorrow when the sun sets."

"No. No. That is not a place for you or me. No," said Jameson.

"Please, please . . . all right, you do not go. Tell me where it is, and I go. Cherokee people go to Charleston all the time. No one will see me. I find Big Dog tied outside the tavern and when no one is looking, I will give her apples. Tell me where it is," she said as her voice grew louder.

Jameson felt stuck between a rock and a hard place. He didn't want to take her but he didn't want her to go alone. He said nothing because he couldn't think what to say.

"Go with me or don't. I do not care. Just tell me where it is!" said Callie, frustrated with his silence.

"Gosh darn it! Dang it! I'll take you. But we won't stay long. You can feed the horse, and then we'll leave. Well, it's an awful bad idea, but I'll take you. We can go the back way into town, and no one will see us. Meet me at the hideaway tomorrow when the sun sets."

"Yes," she said. Before she turned to go home, she motioned to him to give her his hand.

Confused, he lifted his right hand for her to look at. She took firm hold of it and turned it over and back several times.

"Thank you, hand," she said as she released it, grinned, and ran home. Jameson looked back at the tree and the robin, who was now singing.

– 9 –
Why?

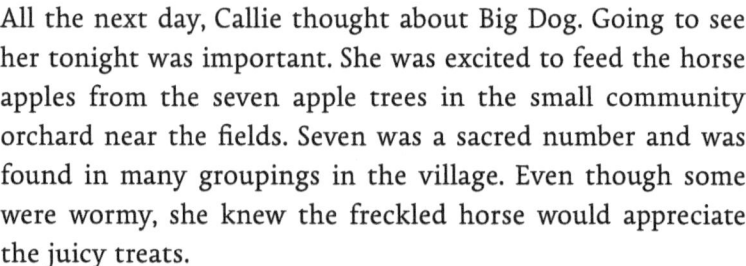

All the next day, Callie thought about Big Dog. Going to see her tonight was important. She was excited to feed the horse apples from the seven apple trees in the small community orchard near the fields. Seven was a sacred number and was found in many groupings in the village. Even though some were wormy, she knew the freckled horse would appreciate the juicy treats.

The real reason she wanted to see Big Dog was to "talk" with Mohe. Callie didn't know or care how this would work but believed that the spirits and ancestors would help. It frustrated her that Jameson didn't understand how crucial seeing Big Dog was. It didn't matter; she only needed him to lead the way. She impatiently watched the yellow sun all day, waiting for it to sink below the horizon.

It was easy for Callie to go out at night. She told Ama she was going to play with the many other village children, chasing each other in a night version of tag. She had a feeling it was not so easy for Jameson, however.

After school that day, Jameson pulled George away from the other children, who were also playing tag outside the schoolhouse. Jameson put his finger to his lips and moved closer to his friend.

"I'm going to tell ma I'm coming over to your house tonight to help you with your math," said Jameson quietly.

"Great!" said George.

"Hey! Quiet. You gotta be quiet because I'm going to tell you something real important. I am not coming to your house—"

George interrupted him. "What? I want you to!"

Jameson continued. "I'm not coming over because I have to take Callie somewhere tonight. I'm mad at her for even asking, but I can't let her go alone. It's dangerous," he said and looked sternly at George. "So, what I have to do is I have to lie to ma and tell her I'm coming to your place."

"Dang. I don't think you've ever lied to your ma. I'd get a big talkin'-to if I lied to my mine, that's for sure. Where are you goin'?" George chewed at his lower lip.

"I'll tell you, but you have to swear on your great-great-grandpa's grave you won't tell anyone," said Jameson, tugging at his black suspender and standing up tall.

"Why do I have to swear on *his* grave? I could swear on my uncle's—"

"It doesn't matter whose grave it is! You can't tell anyone!" said Jameson.

"You don't have to get all hot about it. I won't tell, but I'm sure hopin' no one asks. I don't want to lie and go to Hell," said George.

"No one is goin' to ask, and you ain't goin' to Hell. Well, this is it: I'm going to take Callie to the High Hopes Saloon in town so she can pet that horse. That big white one with brown spots the soldier stole from her friend, same man who kicked King. What a rotten egg he is! I don't rightly know why this is so almighty important to her. It's all bad news. I'm just sayin' to you—I'm tellin' ma I'm coming to your house tonight. So, if my ma ever says anything about all this mess, you gotta say I was at your house."

"But *my* ma will know you weren't there. I don't want to do it," said George, looking at his feet.

"Nothin's gonna happen to anyone. Your ma isn't going to ask about me. I'm just sayin' this, in case. I'm just as mad as you are about havin' to do this, I can tell you that."

"All right. I'll tell a lie for you, but I'm prayin' I don't have to." He looked up at Jameson. "You're with Callie all the time! What about me? Come to my house and tell her not to go," said George.

"I told her! She hears, but she doesn't listen, stubborn as a mule." Jameson turned and walked away while George stared after him.

As soon as the sun slid beneath the pink horizon, Callie pulled a blue, fringed blanket around her, said goodbye to Ama, Waya, and Little Wolf, who was idly playing with his top, and walked out the door. She thought it best to not tell Ama about the hideaway as she didn't know what her grandmother would think about her playing with two white boys. The second she was out of sight, she sprinted to the hideaway to find Jameson already there.

"Let's go!" she said.

"This is dangerous, and I don't want to take you. I don't care if you go. *You* just go," said Jameson. He was batting at a scraggly bush with a stick. A few birds were chirping their night songs.

This surprised her because she thought he agreed that he would take her.

"I go. Yes, I go fine without you. You stay here and ... and play games by yourself. Goodbye," she said but didn't move.

"Well, ain't you goin'?" Jameson asked. Callie saw the smirk on his lips in the dying sunlight.

"Yes. I am. I am going now," she said and mimicked his smirk.

"You don't know where to go! You need me to take you, but I don't feel like it," said Jameson. He spat on the ground for emphasis.

Callie was quiet. She didn't like this new "game" and didn't know how to play it. She wanted to see Big Dog. Callie had ridden her many times with Mohe around the village and to the fields. She would often step sideways instead of going forward, and if she wanted to stop and eat grass, her head went down, and she ate. It was almost impossible to get her to move if she didn't want to. Callie wanted to see her and needed some connection to Mohe as she still felt guilty for not telling Waya what Mohe was planning. She turned away from Jameson and, after a moment, found the path that John Payne had ridden on when he saw them at the hideaway.

Jameson sighed. "Come on. That's the wrong way," he said. "We have to go the back way into town. Follow me."

Jameson led her to a narrow path through the brush. They walked in silence. After a short time, Callie could see the path led directly toward the lights of Charleston. Street gaslights were a newfangled invention, and the town had only six of them mounted on tall wooden poles on the main street. She thought Charleston looked festive and eerie at the same time with its large, flickering lights.

The various saloons in town were packed full of soldiers, but the High Hopes Saloon stood out from the others in terms of its size and the volume of noise coming from inside. Jameson and Callie crouched low and hid behind the saloon. A loud and slightly out-of-tune piano was being pounded on, and Callie wondered if the player loved or hated the thing. Some soldiers blurted out the words to "My Pretty Jane."

There were no windows at the back of the red brick building, and Callie was curious about what the front looked like. She crept around the side of the free-standing building, pausing at the corner, while Jameson watched anxiously. She peeked around the edge so she could see the entrance. A smile lit up her face as she marveled at the lights everywhere and absorbed the boisterous energy of the saloon.

The green door was wide open, and cigar smoke floated out the door. At first, Callie wondered if there was a small fire inside. She heard the piano player more clearly now and decided that even with all that banging, he loved the instrument. She forgot for a moment why she was there as she became lost in the unfamiliar sights and smells.

Everything she saw awed her; however, one smell sickened her. Alcohol permeated the air. It was as if the sweet scents of the trees and the river had been swallowed up and replaced with a slightly poisonous odor. She knew the smell well. Some men in her tribe traded animal skins for whiskey with the soldiers. It frustrated Waya, and he talked to the young warriors about it. While some listened, others did not. Callie thought they seemed almost possessed by the strange drink, unable to stop its hold. As she stood there, she realized it was the same with some white soldiers.

When the odor flooded her senses, she grabbed the edge of the building and turned to find Jameson. He had followed her and was standing close behind her.

"Oh!" she whispered at finding him so near.

"It's safe. They won't come over here. All those men want to do is drink Pepper Whiskey," he said. She wasn't interested in the names of whiskeys and made a little sound that showed that, even though she could see he was proud of what he knew.

"They're just going to play cards and gamble all night. They'll get drunk and that piano player will get even louder, I expect. Pa talks about this problem at suppertime and gets riled up when the soldiers show up for work the next day. I guess they can't even think straight and complain about their headaches all day long," said Jameson.

Callie knew he was trying to impress her. His voice was

at its normal volume as the men inside the High Hopes couldn't hear anything except their own whoops when they won at cards and their swear words when they lost. The piano drowned out everything, anyway.

She had lost patience. "Where is Shiko Waka?" she asked.

"This way. Follow me," he said. She noticed he was taking long strides and seemed to want her to know he was confident. However, Callie sensed he didn't know where Big Dog was but followed him to the back of the saloon and then around to the opposite side of the building.

"Well, here they are. Sure enough! Exactly what I thought," Jameson said as they came upon eight horses loosely tied to a single, long wooden railing running along the side of the building. Callie was now sure he had just guessed. She knew horses well and stayed far enough behind them so they couldn't kick her if they were spooked. She walked down the line, looking at each one.

It was easy to find Big Dog, who was standing closest to the saloon's swinging doors. She was the largest of the horses and the most muscular.

"Hello, Shiko Waka. Hello, Mohe," Callie said, cooing in Cherokee as she rubbed the horse's belly. "I have apples." The horse turned her big, freckled head in Callie's direction. The lights from the saloon were bright enough so that the horse and Callie could see each other. Callie pulled out an apple from her leather satchel. Holding her hand flat open so the horse didn't accidentally nip it, she presented the first of three red apple treats.

The horse opened her gentle mouth, took the entire apple from Callie, and began chomping it happily. Her thick, white mane bounced up and down every time she crunched the sweet treat. While she was eating, Callie stroked her powerful neck and behind her ears, all the while softly singing. Jameson, who was standing behind the calm group of horses, took in the scene. He heard Mohe's name mentioned often. Tears ran down her face as she sang, asking for forgiveness.

The contrast between Callie's sweet song and the slam of shot glasses on the bar went on for quite a while. Then, voices got louder and angrier. Jameson said, "Come on. We need to go."

"No. You go," said Callie, still mildly frustrated at how much work it had been to get him to take her. She was focused on her purpose.

They both jolted when the open door banged against the wall. Because they were close to the entrance, they saw a man stumble out onto the wooden boardwalk in front of the High Hopes. Callie and Jameson sprinted to the back of the building. Callie peeked around the corner to watch, even though Jameson tugged at her arm.

"You skunk! You take my card money every night. You wait!" the tall man shouted toward the green saloon door before he fell. He got up with wobbly effort, went over to Big Dog, clumsily untied her, and got into the saddle after several attempts. Callie turned to say something to Jameson when she heard the sharp snap of the whip. The horse whinnied, and when Callie looked again, she saw the horse rear up, lifting her front legs a foot off the ground. Big Dog was angry, but responded to the whip when it struck her again. She took off with Payne swaying in the saddle and gripping onto the front of it.

"He is evil, like the *U-ya*," Callie said.

"He is a bad penny, not worth much. My pa calls him a varmint, a rat. We sure enough have to stay away from him. I know he's mean to Big Dog, but we can't do anything now."

Callie's breath slowed slightly when she realized there was nothing to do at the moment. She deeply breathed in the cool night air. She was happy she had at least fed the horse treats and asked for Mohe's forgiveness.

After a minute of silence, Jameson sighed. "Whew-y, that was close."

"It's all right now. *Wado* mean thank you. *Wado* for taking me to see Shiko Waka, Jameson."

He grinned as he listened to Callie's soothing voice. "Well now, I will say that man has a brain cavity so small even a hummingbird couldn't get a proper drink from it." He smiled at her, and she knew he was trying to impress her again with his joke.

Callie looked at him with mild curiosity and glanced up at the rising moon. She had no idea what a hummingbird was.

They got back on the path to Rattlesnake Springs. It was narrow at first, and they walked single file with Jameson in the lead. As they got closer to her village, the path opened, and Callie caught up to him. The crickets chirped their rhythmic melodies. Jameson hadn't ever thought much about the moon, soft white and still, but tonight he realized it was beautiful.

"Do you want to walk by the river? It's only a short way from here," he asked.

"May-be," she said.

"Well then, let's go," Jameson said, as he picked up his pace. The dangerous events at the High Hopes Saloon were still eating at him, and he was thinking about other hazards as well. Events that were coming.

The Hiawassee River was wide and shone brown in the moonlight. Gentle sounds came from it as it lapped against the shoreline. Frogs sang their night songs. They sat on the ground. He didn't know how to start or where he wanted to go in the conversation, but it felt urgent.

"The soldiers are talking about something called 'removal'," he said and glanced at her facial expression.

"What is 'removal'?"

"It means the government wants to make the Cherokee people move off their land and out of their homes," he said. He kept going, but his voice had become quieter, and he spoke more slowly. "The government and selfish people want your land to have as their own. They say your people must move west somewhere."

Callie was quiet for a moment and then replied. "This has been talked about and my uncle has tried to stop it. There are many of us. Maybe it's just talk and will not happen."

"I don't know if this will happen either. I think it's terrible, and so does my family," he said, tugging at his suspender.

"Maybe the soldiers decide to be good. Why? Why do they do this? What have our people done to them?" The sound of the lapping waves seemed to grow louder to her.

Jameson had nothing to say, and they both sensed the river shift. It was treacherous now, not peaceful. It held secrets and whispers. He felt cold and tried to button his thick jacket.

"Give me your hand," she said and took his right hand into hers. "Give me other hand." She wrapped her hands around both of his as he held his hands together in a small ball shape. Her mother had done this when she was cold.

"Maybe it won't happen, maybe . . . I don't want it to happen. I don't want you to go away," he said, staring at the river. Her hands were warm.

"I am afraid. I do not know what to do. I am not strong," she said. Her voice shook.

Jameson wasn't sure he heard her correctly. Not strong? She was the strongest person he knew. It's true she was stubborn, but she also knew what she wanted. She acts, he thought. She gets things done, unlike pa.

"I, I think you—" he said as he gently pulled his hands free.

"Please, quiet now. Listen to the earth. Hold my hands tight."

This time he wrapped his hands around hers, trying to touch each one of her fingers with his embrace, trying to keep each one safe. The sounds of the night came back, and he saw her face relax. He released one of her hands, and holding on to the other, he helped her up. They walked hand in hand, and he saw tears roll down her cheeks in the pretty moonlight.

"Good night," Jameson said as he neared her home. He didn't know what else to say or do.

"*Osto*, good night," she said as she turned to look directly into his blue eyes. "Friend, *o gan ollii*," she said.

– 10 –
Soldiers

The next day, Callie helped Ama in the fields and played with Little Wolf. She didn't want to go to school. Still exhausted from the events surrounding Mohe's death, she spent a good portion of the day singing to herself. That afternoon she left her home and walked about a hundred feet into the woods to pee. The earth was cool and still green, although fallen rust-colored leaves created a soft carpet for her. As she walked back, stirring up the dead autumn leaves into a quiet rustle, she thought she heard thunder. When she looked up, the sky was clear. She soon realized it was the pounding hooves of horses, shaking the earth itself. She asked herself, when did they arrive? Gunshots rang out with crisp pops assaulting her ears, and her hands flew up to protect them.

    Horses splashed at the edge of the river, and others were closer to the homes. Commanding officers on horses shouted orders to the thousands of men from Fort Cass, who had marched confidently into her and the other villages. Confused, she halted. She heard people scream and resist. They sounded more angry than fearful. A father barked orders at his children to run and hide. A mother's voice cried out to her children. Terror had arrived along with the soldiers, all dressed in blue. If the devil was a color, thought Callie, he would be blue. She hid behind a large chestnut tree, even though no one was near her. Her feet felt stitched to the ground, and she could not pull free. She stood like a deer who had become lost, panting and glancing every which way. She wanted the tree's large, twisted trunk to shelter her. But nothing was safe, and she knew why they were there.

Soldiers yelled out, "Guns, guns! Give us your guns and knives!"

Callie saw approximately fifty soldiers working together as one unit, going from house to house, breaking up her small area of Rattlesnake Springs, carving her village into pieces. There were several groups of these men, and a commander on horseback supervised each group. They herded people like cattle toward the center of the town. The Cherokee people used the central plazas for sacred dances to thank the crops for their bounty, among other things. Now, the plaza hosted chaos and trauma.

If the Cherokee people didn't move fast enough or with enough cooperation, the soldiers touched a bayonet to their backs to encourage them. She saw many more soldiers posted around the perimeter of the village to chase down people who ran. And Callie saw people running everywhere. Children fell while parents yanked them up by one arm to keep them going. Young men had no choice but to hand over their weapons with so many soldiers surrounding them. She had never heard the fearless warriors cry out in anguish, and yet even the sky wasn't big enough to hold all the fear now.

Soldiers shouted at her people to collect a few of their belongings, but when the soldiers became impatient, they grabbed the old and young alike and threw them out of their small huts. Sometimes a soldier would give the elderly more time, but not all soldiers had a bit of empathy. If a young boy tried to fight, they might shoot in his direction. Everyone understood the language of a gun. If a young girl tried to break free, they ran her down and captured her. They shaped people into roughly formed lines, and many held nothing but the clothes on their backs.

Callie heard more splashing in the river, even wilder than the sound of the horses' hooves plowing through it. She realized it wasn't coming from horses but from people trying to escape. They would surely drown in the Hiawassee's strong currents. People in the village knew to stay away from the river unless they were getting water, bathing, washing clothes, or fishing. Even fishing could lead to death. A mental picture of Little Wolf's father flashed in front of her. She felt the desperateness of her people in every futile splash.

She saw Lula and Blossom's father being forced out of his home with a bayonet at his back. Lula came out with him, standing next to her father as if she had willed a web to bind them together. Perhaps she thought she would be safe if she nestled as close to him as possible. A soldier on horseback stood guard over their home, and several other people's, including Callie's.

"Get out! Get out, I said!" the man on horseback snapped as if giving orders to a group of unruly soldiers, not to innocent people.

Lula's father moved like his legs were made of wood with Lula in tow, holding her hand tightly. He walked several yards outside his door and halted.

"Stop. Please. I speak English. I am your friend," Lula's father said to the man on horseback. "Run! Run!" he suddenly called out. His wife, who was inside, grabbed Blossom in a quick swoop and ran out the door. The man on the horse easily rode up next to her, reached down, and ripped Blossom from her arms, laughing. He threw the toddler over the saddle in front of him so that she was looking at the ground with his hand on her back.

Callie's hands shook uncontrollably. She stared down at them as if they were not hers.

"Got one!" the soldier cried out to no one in particular in an odd, high-pitched voice.

He trotted his horse into the woods, straight toward Callie. He was only thirty feet from the tree Callie was hiding behind when he pulled the horse up hard to stop her. Blossom was crying loudly. Callie saw the child was poorly balanced on the saddle in front of the soldier. The horse wove back and forth wildly as the drunken-sounding man yanked on the reins, this way and that way. All at once, Blossom fell to the ground with a small thud. There was no more crying. He looked down and muttered under his breath, "One less Injun."

When the horse stood still, Callie immediately recognized it was Big Dog by the proud and graceful way she held her head. The man's voice that sounded like ice was also recognizable. The *U-ya* man had let Blossom fall as if she were a sack of flour. John Payne rode the short distance back to Callie's home.

Her hands stopped shaking now, and she was paralyzed with fear.

"This one next. Get them out of here," Payne ordered his soldiers. Two men hurried to her hut and entered. Payne pulled the horse up tight so she could not move. He peered down into the open door from the saddle.

"Is there a girl in this one?" he asked a tired-looking soldier who was standing in the doorway.

"No, sir."

Waya walked out and stood, dignified. "You are evil. The spirits spit on you. You will carry this harm in your heart until it eats you like the wolf chews the rabbit," he said to Payne.

Sergeant Payne quickly dismounted and shoved his face close to Waya's. "Watch your tongue, old man. None of your kind are worth anything. Move, now!"

Ama's clear, sweet voice was almost lost in the chaos, but Callie picked up her words. "No, no, why are you so wicked? Please. Stop. We have done nothing," Ama said, voice rising.

The young soldier entered the hut and pulled hard at Ama's arm to move her toward the door. She shook loose, knelt, and tried to pick up Little Wolf, but he was running in tiny circles. The boy stopped when she told him to, but he cowered in a corner and would not come to her. She tried to grab clothes, but the soldier yanked her arm again. She could only pick up Little Wolf's bearskin blanket. When the soldier jabbed at Little Wolf's shoulder in frustration to get him out of the corner, the small boy ran outside but tripped and fell. Blood dripped from his nose. Little Wolf stood up, confused. In contrast to his usual boisterous and happy nature, there wasn't a single sound coming from his trembling lips.

People cried out names of family members and friends. Anguish was replacing the fear and anger in their voices. Two thunderous gunshots rang out. Then, it was as if the world had become mute, and sound and movement had halted. After a short time, the screaming started up again, but now a great sadness had been added to the mix of terror. Wails floated into the late afternoon as the soldiers went about their methodical business. She saw small lines of people being forced to combine into a long line, creating a trail. She knew, but could not fully understand that Ama, Waya, and Little Wolf would walk that trail.

It took hours to empty the thirteen villages that made up Rattlesnake Springs, but to Callie, sitting behind the tree the entire time, it seemed like minutes. It was over before she knew it, and her own village was still and ghostly. Only then did her sobs come so hard that she struggled to breathe. Her dream had come true, and the earth truly was growing bones. Her world tumbled and rolled and turned upside down. The evil *U-ya* spirit was everywhere. It had flown into her heart and was ripping it out of her chest. After a while, she gathered a little courage, and her sobs turned to whimpers. But when she tried to stand, her legs wouldn't hold her, and she fell back to the ground in despair.

She lay there throughout the night curled in a ball, going in and out of consciousness, afraid to go home in case the soldiers returned. A lonely owl's call woke her as the sun rose. When she opened her eyes, it felt as if the blinding sun had slapped her. The imagined sound of screams and cries would not leave her ears. A tempest of grief had come out of the sky and had descended on her and her people. She thought she heard Little Wolf calling, "Callie, Callie!" But then she could no longer hear him, and it was like he had fallen off the earth.

A shock wave tore through her when she remembered Blossom. Cautiously, Callie stood. She felt strange, as light as an eagle's feather. She was moving, floating through the dry leaves when she saw the small body. Blossom had landed on her back with her neck at an odd angle. She looked as if she had fallen asleep in a small pile of orange-colored leaves. Callie's tears and whimpers began again as she knelt beside Blossom's body and closed her tiny eyes.

She tried to sing the song about the bees she had sung with Ama in the fields, but no words came from her mouth. If only Blossom would wake up, giggle at the silly song, and suck her thumb. So, instead of singing, Callie hummed and didn't stop until she had no voice.

After several hours, she stood and went home. It looked like the village had seen a tornado. Everywhere were bits of humanity: beads, clothes, small wooden toys, food, and one well-worn moccasin, lonely without the other. Shovels and hoes were strewn about haphazardly in the fields. Chickens wandered around aimlessly, looking for food, pecking at cornbread crumbs scattered on the ground. Horses stood in the corral, some tied up and others pacing, skittish, uneasy. Branches had been knocked off small trees as people were pushed and shoved onto the trail. All around her was confusion and loss. Callie stood at the door of her home, took a deep breath, and entered.

She was surprised. At first glance, it didn't look much different from when she had left it to go into the woods. Things were scattered but mostly there. She wondered at this briefly. How could people disappear into the night without the things they own? What happened to their stories, their ceremonies—their way of life—when they were forced to leave without their belongings?

It was impossible that her family was gone. It could not be true, and they would somehow come back. Her grief was wild and unpredictable as she paced inside. The sacred peace pipe Waya had used to unsuccessfully negotiate with General Scott lay trampled, broken in two, near his bedding. She sidestepped the pipe as if being careful might magically fix it. Her balance was off, though, and she leaned against the log wall for support. Her uncle's playfulness, Ama's wisdom, and Little Wolf's innocent love flashed through her mind. How could she live without them? What would she do? Her entire life had deserted her. One foot before the other was all there was for today. She noticed that her warm buffalo blanket lay exactly as she had left it. She picked it up—it was heavier than she remembered—and carried it into the woods.

Choked sobs fell from her lips and tears dropped from her eyes as she approached the child. As gently as she could, Callie laid her blanket on Blossom. Her face remained uncovered, and Callie sang to her, sang for all the loss and for her own emptiness and fear. Early into the afternoon, Callie sang, and then mid phrase, she stopped and did what she hadn't had the courage to do all day. Before she pulled the bearskin over the child's small, still face, Callie leaned down and kissed Blossom's forehead, and her own family, goodbye.

– 11 –
U-ya

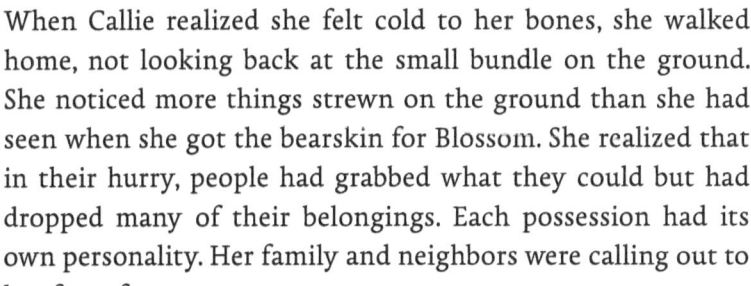

When Callie realized she felt cold to her bones, she walked home, not looking back at the small bundle on the ground. She noticed more things strewn on the ground than she had seen when she got the bearskin for Blossom. She realized that in their hurry, people had grabbed what they could but had dropped many of their belongings. Each possession had its own personality. Her family and neighbors were calling out to her from far away.

Once inside her home again, her body tensed. She was more aware this time. Waya's beautiful hand-carved bow and arrows, which always lay meticulously organized against the wall, had been knocked over. Ama's pan of freshly baked cornbread sat on the small table in the center of the home, but only crumbs were left. Mohe had built birdhouses outside her house for the tree swallows, graceful, swooping birds. She paused and listened but couldn't hear their chirps and whines. Even the beautiful blue swallows had abandoned Rattlesnake Springs.

The terror Little Wolf must have felt pulled at her heart, and she tried with little luck to push it away. His top lay on the floor by his sleeping mat. She picked it up and half-heartedly made it spin. Waya and Ama knew this was coming, but could they have known how destructive it would be?

She imagined her grandmother and uncle walking on the trail, standing tall and sheltering Little Wolf. Perhaps Waya said something courageous to the soldiers after they had formed lines. She knew he had said everything he could to General Scott. Once the soldiers were at their doorstep, was there anything more to say?

The *U-ya* was everywhere, swirling, moaning, and creating chaos. She held her hands over her ears, trying to block him out. Her head hurt, and she was suddenly so tired she could not stand. She crawled onto Ama's bed mat and covered herself with her grandmother's bearskin blanket. Before she fell asleep, in a half dream state, she sat straight up, thinking she was Blossom, warmed but also smothered by the blanket. After calming herself as best she could, she told herself she was alive and fell into a deep sleep.

Midafternoon, she woke up, hungry. She didn't want to be in her sad home anymore, so she grabbed her blue shawl and thought about food. She would come back later and get Little Wolf's top and the arrows and Ama and Waya's bearskin blankets. They would not be lost to her family. And she would make a plan to find her family. But for now, food.

The hideaway. After she had walked for ten minutes, she remembered her necklace and hoped it was still in the little bowl she and her grandmother had made. It sat next to her forlorn sleeping mat, missing its heavy bearskin blanket which now covered Blossom. She paused and nearly turned back but as she was almost at the hideaway; hunger drove her forward. She would get the necklace later.

Callie was surprised to see the boys sitting on the ground outside the hideaway, idly whittling sticks with small pocket knives. When they saw Callie approach, they stood so quickly that when Jameson's knife fell to the ground, it was close, too close, to George's foot. George looked down and then his eyes went right back up to stare at Callie.

"Callie!" exclaimed George. He moved to hug her but stopped short out of embarrassment.

"I . . . what? What happened? Are you all right?" asked Jameson, also on his feet now. "You don't look so good. You look tired. Come inside."

He and George stared at each other in astonishment as Callie went into the hideaway ahead of them. They took their usual places on the tree stump chairs, but she could not get comfortable and shifted back and forth on her chair. She tugged at her braids to make them look more ready for the day, but thick black strands of hair fell into her eyes, and she stopped trying.

"I am hungry," she said without emotion.

"Here, here. You can have my bread and meat. I have an apple too," said George as he walked over to pick up the small basket of food Mary had packed for the boys. Jameson nodded in agreement.

She tore chunks of bread off with her teeth and ate the large piece in five bites. A brief memory of spitting out the strange food George shared with her at school passed through her mind. It had been only a few days ago, but today life was utterly different. She quickly chewed on the dried beef and relaxed as she took a bite of the sweet-tasting apple.

"Well, you sure were hungry!" said Jameson. "We heard soldiers came to Rattlesnake Springs yesterday. Pa stayed at the fort, but he and ma talked about it all morning. It was an awful, sad thing. Where is your family? I can't believe you're here!"

Callie stared at the ground.

"Please, tell us. What happened?" said George.

"I don't know. I was in the woods when the soldiers came. I heard screams and saw people pushed into a line. I can't speak now. I wish for quiet," she said.

"Do you want to play Marbles?" George asked with no energy. He pointed to the marbles in the purple reed basket Callie had made for them, hoping she would change her mind.

"No," she said.

King popped into the hideaway, tail wagging. It seemed to Callie that he sensed her sadness and walked over to her. She looked down at his scruffy face, too-big nose, and sparkling black eyes. A small smile took hold of her. After licking her hand, he lay down at her feet. She got off her tree stump and sat on the ground by him, petting his mangy, curly, black-and-white fur.

There was a long silence while Callie petted King. She spoke tenderly. "King-er, good dog. Nice dog," she said as she lifted his head to look into his eyes. He gave her face a big lick, and she smiled at George.

George bit his lower lip. "Where is Lula?"

A wave of pain hit Callie between her eyes. Lula had been marched by the soldiers somewhere. She was gone. Everyone on that trail was. And Blossom was dead.

"She is walking with all the people. I don't know more."

"Where did everyone go?" asked George. "I mean, where did they make your people go?" he said softly.

Jameson, too, looked at her, his lips twitching. "I'm glad you're here. That's all that matters right now. I'm sorry, so sorry this happened." Callie said nothing.

Jameson said more loudly, "We've asked enough questions for now. King is here, so you have to go home, George. Do you have math tonight?"

"I always have math and sums! And tonight is even a worser night than usual. I have to take a bath, too, and that water gets darned cold. There's not a speck of dirt on me ... well, except for my knees and fingernails, but that's just normal dirt! That's nothin' that needs to be scrubbed off because it'll just come back on me tomorrow," said George. He stood, but his shoulders drooped.

"Well, I'm sorry about all those problems. But let's think, George. Me having to plow through my dull, old book and you having to scrub your knees sure enough isn't anything compared to what Callie's been through." After a pause, he continued. "And don't mention Callie is here to your parents. We have to understand this whole situation better," he said, glancing sideways at her.

By now, King had left Callie's side and was nuzzling George's leg.

"I guess I won't. This is a terrible mess. Aw, I have to go," said George. "Tomorrow is Sunday, so I have to go to church and pray all day, which is downright boring. Callie, will you come to school on Monday? But now that I think of it, is that safe?"

He patted King on the back and added, "I sure am sorry about all of this. I will pray for you and your family and your friends and your neighbors and all the Cherokee people. And I'm goin' to pray especially good for Lula and her little sister, Blossom, right? Is that her name? Whew! That'll sure enough be the most prayin' I've ever done!" He and King left, running side by side.

Callie wept, her head shaking gently back and forth. Jameson looked at her, not knowing what to do. He knew the enormity of what had happened was settling in and the aloneness must be holding her hostage. He saw her breathing become shallower and her expression change as she drifted into a land of waking nightmares.

"I'm here. I'm right here. See? You're safe. Tell me whatever you want to, or you don't have to say anything," he said. He sounded confident, but his neck tightened. He rubbed it.

She motioned for him to get off his tree stump and sit by her on the ground. He quickly moved to her side and waited and waited. He could see out the open door that the sun was sinking low in the sky. He'd need to go home soon.

Looking directly in front of her but not at Jameson, she began.

"I went to the woods to pee. On my way back, I hear people shouting." Jameson inched closer to her side.

"I saw my home from behind a tree. I could not see everything but some things. I heard Ama cry out and her big voice was so little. I was afraid. I could not help anyone. I saw Little Wolf fall to the ground, but Waya was proud and strong."

She needed to tell her story, to get it out of her. She spoke more rapidly.

"A man on a horse came by the tree, and I heard his *U-ya ice* voice. He had something on his saddle, sitting in front of him. It was Blossom, Lula's little sister. She fell, and he didn't care. It was the bad man who took Shiko Waka. I know his voice. He rode away."

Jameson sat, stunned, blinking quickly. "Is she all right?"

"No. She is dead."

Jameson breathed in hard and looked down.

"I stayed by the tree a long time and when all the people were gone, I went to her, and her neck is wrong. I tried to sing her the Bee Song. Do you know this song?" Callie turned to look at him as if she just remembered that Jameson was there. He thought that until then she had been talking almost to herself.

"No, no. I don't know this song. I . . . I wish I did. Blossom liked it?" he said.

"Blossom love it. So, I sing it to her for a long time. But she did not wake up. I covered her with my blanket. She is alone in the woods, so alone. But she has my blanket to keep her warm now." Callie was out of words.

Jameson said nothing. He was astonished that this had happened, that the United States government had so much power they could tell an entire group of people to move to some unknown place. That they couldn't take their belongings. That their land would be stolen. That his father could do nothing.

"Where are they going?" he asked. His voice was barely louder than a whisper.

"I don't know. They went west, toward the setting sun." His body heat warmed her.

"How will they get there?" he asked. His eyes narrowed, and he shook his head in confusion.

"I don't know. I think they will walk. And weak people will die if they must walk a long way. I am worried about my grandmother and brother. They are not so strong." Jameson saw tears gather in her eyes.

After a moment, Callie started up again. Her face was flushed with excitement. "I can catch them! Yes, I can go after them and catch up to them!"

"What? What are you saying? They are in danger, and at least you are safe now," Jameson said and instinctively put his arm around her shoulder. She shook free of it.

"I don't care about safe. I need my family. I will go after them. I start now." She jumped up. Jameson stood too. "I go now," she said.

"You will never catch up with them. They are a day's walk ahead. You can't catch them. Stay. We will figure something out. Please," he said.

Callie ignored him, and her eyes brightened. "You are right. Too far away now. But I can catch them with a horse. I can catch them with Big Dog! We will take Big Dog tonight. She will be at the saloon. We will go like we did the other night, but tonight I will untie her. And then I will leave. Big Dog and I will find my family. I only want to be with them. I do not care if it is dangerous."

This time Jameson did not argue but pointed out that soldiers don't go to the saloon every night. Maybe the man wouldn't be there. Nevertheless, he would help and he would lie again to his mother. He would say he was going to George's, and his mother would believe him. Everything about this was wrong, but there was no right plan. He wanted her to be happy.

"Stay here," he said. "I will be back soon, and we'll go to the saloon."

"I will. I will be here," she said. "Please bring food."

If he could have, he would have brought her every single thing there was to eat in his mother's kitchen.

– 12 –

Cards

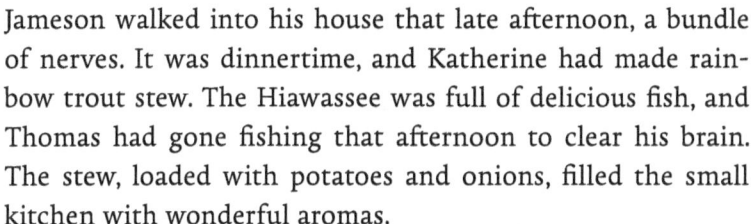

Jameson walked into his house that late afternoon, a bundle of nerves. It was dinnertime, and Katherine had made rainbow trout stew. The Hiawassee was full of delicious fish, and Thomas had gone fishing that afternoon to clear his brain. The stew, loaded with potatoes and onions, filled the small kitchen with wonderful aromas.

"What have you been doing this afternoon? The sun is setting earlier now," his mother asked Jameson.

"Well, me and George were just whittlin' sticks," he said. Feeling shaky, he sat down heavily, and the chair creaked.

"It's George and I, not me and George, dear," she said while dishing up the stew. There were three large, heavy, brown ceramic bowls on the table, along with a simple, woven basket of warm bread. As Jameson's mouth watered in anticipation, he remembered Callie's request. She was hungrier than he was.

Thomas was quiet as she filled the bowls. She spilled a bit of stew on the table and wiped it up in one swipe with her apron. Three white candles in pewter holders bathed the table in soft light. After the evening meal prayer, she talked with her husband in a strained voice.

"I know you're thinking about the removal. It's a true sin what we did to our Cherokee neighbors. But it's done. It's done now. We did what we could. There's nothing more to do."

"I tried not to be a part of it, Kathie. I told William he needed to stay at the fort, and I know Mary is thankful for that. The general wanted me on horseback at the head of one of the long lines, lines that were miles long. Thousands of Cherokee people and thousands of soldiers converging onto that hellish trail! There is no doubt that people will die. We don't have enough food or other supplies for them. I was supposed to lead people west on my horse, holding the American flag high! But I told the general it was better for me to stay behind and manage the fort, be on the lookout for escapees. The general thought about it, and in the end, James Wayland led. I managed affairs at the fort and was not the least bit interested in escapees," said Thomas.

Escapee! Was Callie an "escapee," thought Jameson.

"I know. I know, dear," said Katherine. His left hand was resting on the table, and she put hers on top of it.

Jameson didn't know his father had ever told General Scott "No." For a moment, he was relieved he had stood up to the general, but fury at his father's inability to put an end to the removal soon rushed back.

"Well, I guess you didn't have to lead the people, Pa, but it didn't work! Did it? You still couldn't stop it!" said Jameson who slammed his spoon on the table. Thomas looked at him and set his own spoon down, carefully and controlled.

Katherine said, "You're right. Your father could not stop people from being dragged from their homes. Mary said she heard the lines were an odd combination of silence and sobbing. Stunned, that is what the Cherokee people were. Traumatized, walking to God knows where. It's a monstrous thing and something your father and others could not stop." Her face softened and tears welled up in her eyes.

Thomas picked up his spoon and took a bite of stew, watching her. She continued. "And I told you that I wrote letters to Congress along with a great number of other women, and Mary and I have prayed together every night for the past week. We pray for strength for the Cherokee people, that they might rise above this injustice. That they might show us what courage looks like, because this removal is an act of cowardice on our part." Katherine closed her eyes for a few seconds and breathed deeply through her nose.

Thomas looked up from his bowl and sat up straighter in his chair. "Son, you are right but also wrong. And while I understand your anger, you will speak to me more politely in the future. I, your mother, and many others could not stop it. But it matters that we did something. Doing nothing was not a choice. We did what we could."

Jameson didn't know how he felt. His face was hot and flushed, and he wasn't sure that doing "something," when the result was still bad, mattered. However, he also understood that doing nothing could have meant his parents supported the removal. At least he was clear on that one thing. He knew they had taken action. He remembered that Callie said Waya had tried, too, when he talked with General Scott and his father. When Jameson began to eat his stew again, he thought of Callie.

"I don't want to talk about this anymore. I'm going to George's after dinner. He has a lot of math he needs help with. You know that, Ma," he said, hoping to sound nonchalant about his lie.

"You were just there. Does he still need help?" she asked, raising her eyebrows.

"He sure enough does. Well, he can't seem to get the idea of multiplication. Like you say, we must keep practicing our problems," Jameson said, scraping his spoon on his near-empty bowl.

"That's it. That is how you learn math. I'm glad you're helping him. He's certainly a nice friend," she said.

Jameson felt his stomach tighten. He didn't like to lie and hadn't until lately. He sat, unsure what to do next.

"Will you take a bowl of fish stew and bread to Mary? She's

been asking me how to make this stew, and one good way to learn how to make something is to eat it," Katherine said.

Jameson couldn't believe his luck. "Sure, Ma," he said.

As she put the stew and bread together in a picnic basket for Jameson, he stood waiting by the door. Impatient. When it was finally ready and covered with a red-and-white checked cloth, a ripple of gratitude for her kindness unexpectedly overtook him. That was followed by a stronger wave of something like fear for what he was about to do. He started to walk out the door when his father called his name. He turned around.

"I want you to know we especially prayed for Callie and her family," he said.

Jameson nodded his head "Thank you" but then thought that his ma and pa better start praying a lot harder.

Callie choked a little when she took such a big bite of bread. Not sure about the thick, milky fish stew, Callie dipped the next piece of bread cautiously into the rich mixture. It disappeared even faster than the setting sun.

"Hey, slow down!" Jameson said. "That fish isn't going anywhere!"

Callie laughed a little. "*Wado,* thank you. We go now. Now we go to Shiko Waka," she said and wiped her chin with the back of her hand. She did not want to argue with or be stopped by him this time. In her mind, she could hear Little Wolf's cries of delight when she would pull him into her arms.

"I know. We'll go," Jameson said in a shaky voice.

It had started raining while they were inside talking. They got on the muddy path to the High Hopes Saloon, not saying anything the entire way into town. A few times they took refuge under large oak trees, waiting for the cold rain to let up. Callie suddenly felt sad that while she would join her family, she would also leave this life behind. She pulled her shawl tightly around her shoulders and tied it into a sturdy knot in front so it would stay in place for the long night ahead of her. Jameson had on a thick, gray-flecked wool jacket, and he buttoned it up. A chill was moving in with the sun gone.

Her plan was to get Big Dog, go home, pack a few things, and head west. She knew her people would sleep on the trail that night on the ground, covered by blankets if they had been able to take them. She would ride through the night. That would be the best way to catch up with them.

Soon Callie saw the flickering gas streetlamps of Charleston. The piano player pounded away, and his music sailed through the air as they neared the High Hopes Saloon. It was Saturday night, and the place was filled with boisterous soldiers. Callie and Jameson stood by the outside rear wall of the saloon, listening. They heard men singing, which sounded more like shouting. Between demands for "another" shot of whiskey and arguments over poker, she realized the card players sounded good-natured most of the time. Unexpectedly, someone's anger boiled over, and she heard chairs smack onto the wood plank floor.

Callie forced her attention away from all the racket and walked directly to the side of the saloon where the horses were tethered. Jameson followed, his feet sounding heavy to her as he slowly picked them up, one after another. She was impatient with him. Big Dog was tied to the railing in the same position she had been before, nearest to the saloon doors. She was pawing nervously in the mud, bothered by the sounds and lights. Callie walked up to her, cooing. "Hello, Shiko Waka. Tonight, we will ride together."

Before she could untie the lead rope that was looped over the railing, the green saloon door slammed open and then swung back shut with a bang. She and Jameson froze in place and saw a short, drunk man stumble out of the bar and onto the boardwalk. He didn't fall but looked like he would at any minute. He disappeared around the other side of the tavern, and they heard a sharp yelp.

"Let's get out of here. Untie Big Dog, and let's go," said Jameson in a hushed voice. He began to untie the lead, fumbling with it in his hurry.

"Leave her. We will go, but I want to see this man. He is hurt," she said. She pushed his hands away from the rope.

"No, Callie. You don't know what these men are like. He's drunk. He's probably passed out on the ground. His friends will find him later tonight. Untie Big Dog," said Jameson.

She ignored him and walked around the back of the building to the other side. Low moaning was coming from bushes near the saloon. She moved closer and saw that the man had hit his head when he slipped on the slick, muddy ground. He lay face up, eyes rolled back.

Jameson had followed and stood behind her, anxiously looking around for trouble. Callie peered down at the whimpering man, wondering what to do. The saloon door opened again but quietly and with care this time. The slow click of boot heels moved toward them. Jameson and Callie crept deeper into the brush to hide. John Payne's head slowly swept from side to side as if he were trying to locate something. The man on the ground made a deep moaning sound like a poor, wounded animal, Callie thought. The tall man stepped off the boardwalk and swiftly moved toward the soldier on the ground. He knelt to look at the soldier's face.

"Ain't you in a fine mess, you worthless snake? Hit your head? I didn't play poker with you tonight, so no one will suspect me. Sick of you takin' my money. I'm takin' it back and then some," said Payne in a low growl.

The piano played on, but Callie and Jameson could hear and see him as they were only fifteen feet away, hidden behind large, still leafy green shrubs. Payne knelt and reached into the downed soldier's coat pocket.

The wounded man woke up when he felt someone poking around in his coat pocket. "What . . . what the hell?" he said as he grabbed the tall man's arm. Payne shook free, hesitated, and then put his enormous hands around the injured soldier's neck. He tightened them and did not let go. The soldier, weakened by his fall and whiskey, fought back, ineffectively swatting at the relentless, determined hands. Soon enough, the man stopped fighting and lay still.

In the lights of the saloon and the streetlamps, Callie could see John Payne release his grip and reach back into the dead man's jacket, pulling out a wad of bills before he stood. It outraged her. All fear had left her. Her anger at what had happened to her people and Payne's treatment of Mohe and Big Dog rose inside her like a swirling storm. Abruptly, she stood up and moved toward him. Jameson, shocked, also stood and grabbed Callie's arm, trying to pull her back under cover. Payne heard the bushes rustle and turned his head toward the sound. Jameson glanced at him in fear and confusion.

Callie, however, stood firm, looking him square in the eyes. She would face the *U-ya*. He moved a few steps toward the brush to see who was hiding there. The saloon lights shone through the windows and spilled onto Callie and Jameson. Payne was disoriented for a second and slid in the black slush mud but caught himself. With ice-cold eyes, he returned Callie's stare. He let out a grunt. "Keep your mouths shut, you little bastards." Callie and Jameson watched as he walked, almost strolled, around the back of the bar to the other side where the horses were. Callie panicked and, desperate to get Big Dog, ran after him.

Jameson caught up to her and tugged at her arm, firmly this time. "No. Stop," he said.

She pulled loose and took another five steps before they both heard it. The whip snapped into the brisk air. It cracked again and then once more. An angry whinny called out in the dark and then the sound disappeared into the night.

"We have to go. Come on, we have to go," said Jameson, out of breath. She followed him back onto the path out of town. They ran at first but slowed to a walk when Jameson realized he didn't know where to go or what to do next. He didn't want Callie to sense his fear. He could see that rage was still surging through her and fright hadn't set in. Jameson slowed down.

"You must tell your father. You go home now and tell him about this man. He killed a soldier! He is a killer! Your father can help. Please, Jameson," she said. Her voice cracked. "I'm tired of talking in your words." She began to speak in her own language, fluid and smooth.

"What?" he mumbled, still in shock. He took a step back from her.

"Tell your father!" she said, louder. She grabbed the front of his gray wool coat with both hands and shook him.

Jameson's mind raced. He felt as if he was going to fall, and his stomach tightened like someone had punched him in the gut. His father was useless: he could not stop the removal, couldn't stop the hanging, nothing. Weak. And his mother had told him not to see Callie. Neither of them knew she had escaped the removal. He had lied repeatedly. His head felt like someone was holding him underwater or like Payne was strangling him.

Yet, he knew he had to tell his father what happened. But not tonight, maybe tomorrow. If the United States government was so mighty and strong to push around an entire town of innocent people, they'd figure out it was Payne soon enough, he thought. Jameson didn't want to be involved, and he was afraid of Payne and his retribution. If he just waited, maybe everything would sort itself out without him.

"I will. I will tell pa. That's right. That's the right thing. Maybe tomorrow. The soldiers will figure out who it was, anyway. But for now, we can't say anything to anyone. Do you hear me? We can't tell George or anyone. I'll take care of it. I'll figure something out," he said.

"Tell your father now!" Callie said. Mohe's words to her, "Don't tell anyone," flashed through her mind. It was happening again. She shook him again. "Please!"

"All right, all right. I will," he lied. He needed time, time to come up for air.

She relaxed her grip and dropped her hands to her sides. "I will sleep at the hideaway. I do not want to go home. It's lonely there," said Callie as tears welled up. He saw her anger change to sadness. He knew that if she didn't start on the trail soon, she wouldn't catch up to her family.

"Yes. Let's go there," Jameson said, seeing at least one step forward.

They walked in silence through the chilly night, stars and moon prominent in the late October sky. When they got to the hideaway, it was warmer inside. The wind was kept out by the sturdy log walls the boys had smeared with mud. Along with candles, the tree stump chairs, and the game equipment tossed in a corner, the thick, gray wool blanket from Mary's store lay loosely folded in another corner.

"I go to sleep," she said as she laid the blanket on the ground for her bed. She untied her shawl and rested on her side, pulling her long deerskin dress toward her feet for warmth. Her tan, shin-high moccasins with their red beads wiggled to find a comfortable spot. At last, she draped her small shawl across her legs and torso, leaving her arms exposed.

Jameson had been watching quietly from his seat on the stump. When she rested her head on her folded arm, he rose to leave, but stopped and took off his thick wool jacket. He'd tell his mother he left it at George's. He knelt and covered her arms with his coat.

She raised her head slightly to look at him. "*Wado* and *osto*, thank you and good night," she whispered before lying back down and closing her eyes.

– 13 –

Relief

The next morning Jameson and his family walked a mile to town dressed in their Sunday best. His mind was cluttered and confused, and he doubted church would help. He was worried about Callie and tried to get out of it, but Katherine insisted. So, he brushed off his muddy boots, pulled them on, and headed out the door with his parents.

The Episcopalian church was the largest, and therefore, the most important of the three churches in Charleston. It was painted white and the five stairs leading up to the sanctuary were framed with elaborate metal railings. Set just outside of town in a grassy area, the enormous cross on the top of the building invited sinners in for forgiveness. Jameson trudged up the stairs, head down.

After yesterday's rain, the morning sun shone its face through the clear glass windows. A large, light-colored wood podium, where the minister delivered his fiery speeches, stood dead center at the front of the church. Behind that, hanging on the wall was something spectacular that always impressed Jameson. At twelve feet tall, the plaster statue of "Jesus on the Cross" dominated the sanctuary with its sorrowful colors. Blood dripped from Jesus's head, hands, and feet, made more distinctive against the pure white cross. Jameson closed his eyes briefly, thinking about his many lies.

As the church bells rang out, people filed into the pews. They were neighborly, and there were many greetings and "good mornings." Thomas, Katherine, Jameson, George, and his mother and father filled half a bench in the center of the room. The officers from the fort, in full dress uniform, were required to go to church whether or not they believed in that statue. A shudder ran through Jameson when he saw John Payne enter and sit in the back row. He had a bored, surly look and was picking at his nails.

At the end of the long service, several parishioners made community announcements. Mrs. Enright let everyone know that there would be pie and coffee for sale on the church lawn. There was a stirring in the crowd, and Jameson wondered if they were looking forward to the pie or just to get outside away from the minister's booming voice. More announcements followed, and finally, General Scott stood. People, even John Payne, stopped wiggling and sat at attention.

"I would like the good people of Charleston to know that last night there was a murder of one of Fort Cass's finest soldiers. We are in full control of the situation and will find the murderer. There is no reason you decent folks should be concerned. But if any of you hear news about this, please come to me immediately. I believe you'll find me and my headquarters warm and welcoming." He began to sit but changed his mind and rose again. "And, I also have excellent coffee."

Jameson squeezed his eyes shut and tried to calm his churning mind. Hearty laughter as well as concerned murmurs rippled through the church. Jameson quickly glanced at the rear of the church and saw Payne, who now looked almost asleep. His mother nudged at him to turn around.

He knew the people of Charleston and the farmers were relieved Fort Cass was nearby, and they felt protected by the soldiers. There had been few problems with the people in Rattlesnake Springs, but everyone in church knew about the removal and had been watching with anticipation as more men in uniform arrived. Jameson had sometimes seen women give a friendly nod to a Cherokee child riding on a horse with her father, sitting securely in front of him on the thick saddle blanket. But there was not much connection beyond that. It made Jameson angry that most of the community was happy the Cherokee people had finally been removed.

Preacher James, who had stepped away from the podium for the announcements, moved back to it with a swish of his long, white robe, draped in a piece of black fabric around his neck. He looked like a man of opposites to Jameson: white-and-black robe, the good and bad, the right and wrong of life. And he knew the preacher intended to teach his flock what he thought were the right ways.

"I have a final announcement, good citizens. The United States government sent me a letter recently." He held up a formal-looking piece of paper. "With the removal of the Cherokee and with the move to their new home out west, and so I've heard is wonderful, our government is hard at work preparing the details for our new land purchases. I have also heard that the Cherokee have taken good care of their land, and so you will find yourselves fortunate to farm it. If I may, I'd like to let you all in on a little secret." He put his finger to his lips and whispered, "Shhh." Jameson thought he looked silly.

The parishioners were quiet and attentive. "The government has assured me that the land will be sold to you for an extremely reasonable, dare I say low, price."

The crowd clapped enthusiastically and smiled at each other.

"Outside, all! I will have another grand announcement there. First, pie and coffee!"

The rustle of long Sunday dresses in bright colors filled the sacred space as people rose. People walked out in an orderly fashion, row by row, but friendly chatter was everywhere. Handshaking was in no short supply. Thomas and his family walked by John Payne on the way out, and it startled Jameson to see Payne sitting stiff as a board, staring directly at him as he passed by. Once everyone was on the lawn, they spread out in the sunshine. Lines formed for the pies. He thought of the terrible lines Callie described.

Jameson wasn't hungry for the renowned rhubarb pie or for any pie. His stomach had been upset since the events of last night. He stood alone, away from the crowd. Payne moved toward him, assured and quickly with long strides.

"I saw you last night. You and that Injun girl. You keep your damn mouths shut or you'll both pay." His words were quiet and fast, and as he spoke, he inched toward Jameson.

Then, Payne turned and walked away as suddenly as he had arrived. Jameson glanced at the boisterous crowd and vomited onto the short prairie grass.

Preacher James again took center stage behind the pie table filled with at least thirty plump, delicious-looking pies of all sorts. "May I have your attention? Please, may I have your attention?!" he shouted, waving his hands. The crowd became hushed. "Here we go! I have received permission in the letter I presented to you earlier to hold a lottery. The government is pleased to offer one parcel of Cherokee land, ten acres, absolutely free to the winner!"

Cheers rose into the crisp air. Even the children, not understanding the idea but feeling the excitement, ran around faster in their games of tag. Jameson had walked over to his parents to be near their safety. Thomas and Katherine, who were standing and sipping coffee, looked at each other and shook their heads. Thomas leaned over and said to her, "Oh, Lord, no. How insulting can we be to these people?"

The minister held the lottery, and farmer Davis was the winner. He strode up to the preacher to shake his hand. The congregation heartily congratulated him, and most smiled, seeming to believe he and his family were well deserving of the free land. But Jameson noticed a few people who looked as though they wished they had won.

"With the Cherokee gone, we can feel safe, yes, reassured, for ourselves but also for them," Pastor James said. "I understand they are a happy and grateful people. Simple-minded, though, and give too much attention to ancestors and nature. I digress, what a glorious new beginning we shall have! The government makes no mention of what to do with the things the Cherokee left behind. They're probably not worth much, but if you wish, you might go see what is left in Rattlesnake Springs. No use letting it rot away before we occupy our new land."

Jameson saw people move out of the yard in all different directions. They talked about going home to get their horses to carry things. Some had buggies pulled by horses already waiting outside the church. Rattlesnake Springs was only a forty-minute walk away. Although it was close, few people and not even their community leader, Preacher James, had ever been there. Jameson knew most of them had never been inside a Cherokee home. It frustrated him that the hunger for things unknown pulled at even the best of them.

Not all townsfolk believed it was right. There were those who stayed back and continued to sip their coffee. They soon walked home, and Jameson heard a man say that he would pray for the safety of the Cherokee people. There were a few soldiers, too, who left in pairs to return to the fort, seeming to not see any good in taking even more from the Cherokee.

"This is a sorry sight. A sorry day, Kathie. Let's go home," said Thomas.

"Yes. The pie tastes sour now."

"Jameson, are you sick? You look pale," said George. They had both stayed behind when their parents went home. He continued even though Jameson ignored him. "Do you want to play tag?"

"No, I want to be alone."

"I'll be darned. I do believe something is wrong with you."

"Go away. Leave me be," said Jameson.

George answered, "Nope. Not until you tell me what's wrong. Nope!"

"Well, you can't tell anyone. Promise . . . promise?" said Jameson, lowering his voice. He was bursting inside to tell someone something. And George was in front of him.

"Yep. I'm real good at secrets. That's the best thing about me is keeping secre—"

Jameson interrupted him. "Last night, Callie and I went to Charleston, to the High Hopes Saloon."

"Again? Why? Good Lordy! You were there a few nights ago with her. She wanted to see the horse that soldier stole from her friend, right? He sure is a rotten snake," George said.

"She wanted to get Big Dog back and catch up to her family. She didn't think they would be far along because they're walking. I had to help her, but it didn't work out. It did not work out at all."

"Wasn't Big Dog there? Why are you letting Callie go? It's not safe for her to go out on that trail all alone," said George, chewing on his lower lip.

"The horse was there, and I don't want Callie to go. But what can I do? I tried to talk her out of it, but no way did she listen. I didn't know what else to do. So, I took her to the saloon. But it went wrong, and she slept at the hideaway last night."

George quickly asked, "What happened? Is this the secret part?"

"We saw something. It was real bad, a real bad thing happened. I can't say more. I just can't."

"Did you tell your pa about it?" said George.

"No. Pa can't or won't do anything about anything. He couldn't stop Callie's family and her entire village, her whole damn village from being forced out of their homes."

George scrunched up his eyes. "I've never heard you use cuss words, but you have to tell your pa. You just do."

"Maybe I will tell him something about it, maybe soon. I know I have to. I'm going to get some food at home, and I'll meet you at the hideaway this afternoon. Callie is there alone. I'm worried about her." Jameson glanced in the direction of the hideaway. "You said it's not safe to let her go. But you are sure enough wrong. It's not safe to let her stay."

When Jameson saw the long line of excited people heading toward Rattlesnake Springs after church, he and George went home. He didn't want to see their greed or hear their happy chatter. George mentioned how relieved he was that Callie didn't have to witness the theft that was about to take place, and Jameson slowly nodded in agreement.

In some ways, it resembled the long line of people who were forced out of Rattlesnake Springs two days before. But the mood of the two groups was very different. Gaiety versus sorrow. Expectation versus dread. Hope versus loss. Hungry and dazed chickens greeted the mob of parishioners. The chickens wandered aimlessly everywhere, even inside the now-empty homes.

Because Callie's hut was on the outskirts of the village, it was one of the first to be looted. Others in her area were also full of people in no time. Three or four townspeople were inside each hut, rummaging through things while others waited and peered into the open doors. There was a general din of "oh"s and "ah"s as people found things they had never seen. The women were interested in the cooking utensils and immediately saw the value of the beautiful pottery that held dried beans and other food. The colorful and intricately woven baskets were especially fascinating. There was a considerable amount of chatting among the women as to possible uses for the baskets.

The men moved into the fields to examine the slash-and-burn farming techniques used by the Cherokee. Many had heard about the method and knew it to be especially successful with the three sister crops: corn, beans, and squash. The Cherokee farmers were masters at cutting down thick forests around the edges of the village, burning the grass and weeds, and transforming the soil into rich farmland. They were aware of how often to do this so that the land was not overused and depleted. Even though it was fall and the Cherokee had harvested the plants, the farmers walked among the fields to study and marvel at the new method.

Grazing cattle, sheep, and goats seemed unburdened by the events of two days ago. They wandered from here to there, heads down to munch grass, heads up to take stock of their surroundings. The settlers devised a system among themselves of who would take which animal. One of the most successful community farmers announced he would manage the process, and he would do it "with fairness".

All the men, both farmers and townspeople, were interested in the corral. Twenty horses got left behind in Callie's village. Anxious, hungry, and some still tied to the split-rail fence, they turned their heads from side to side as the men approached. The Cherokee horses, mostly brown or tan with white or black splashes of color, were a high-strung breed. They held their heads proudly and were quick to notice their surroundings. But today, their eyes were full of fear and confusion.

Three soldiers arrived at the corrals first and had already decided on the horses they would personally take. When the townsmen arrived, the soldiers announced the horses were off-limits. They were now the property of Fort Cass. Disappointed men, one or two trying to argue, slumped away. The three soldiers slapped each other on the back. They had successfully kept all the horses for themselves and for the fort. Although there were no formal orders to do so, they were certain they would be greeted as clever heroes by General Scott.

Two women with large sun hats tied under their chins with blue ribbons, entered Lula's hut. They took a few things, but it had mostly been picked over by the time they arrived. They moved on to Callie's home, where they found three baskets of different sizes that held Ama's best healing herbs, including wild ginger, yarrow, and hummingbird blossoms. The women didn't know what the herbs were used for, but they admired the delicate brown and tan weaves in the baskets. One of them took each basket outside and dumped out the herbs behind the hut, watching for a moment as they blew away on the breezy day. While she was doing that, her friend discovered Little Wolf's top.

"Oh, this is nice. Isn't it? I didn't know they made things this well. Did you? Look, it works perfectly," she said as she spun it around and around on the floor. "Why, my little Henry will love this! I'd have to say I'm the winner today, Sarah," she said as they both strolled out laughing.

The crowd was thinning. They had picked over the useful items. John Payne had been pacing in the area, back and forth, in and out of a few homes, waiting. He wanted to get into Callie's home. It was empty now. He ducked his head slightly to enter. Once inside, he stood and looked around. He saw things overturned, broken, and two bearskin blankets crumpled up. The sleeping mats were intact as the villagers had no use for them. He wasn't looking for anything special. Curious. Something colorful caught his eye at the top of one of the three mats.

A small, overlooked, blue-striped pottery bowl sat on the ground. Bending down, he picked it up. In it was Callie's orange beaded necklace. His lips curled into a small smile as he shoved it into a torn pocket of his dark blue military jacket. He dropped the bowl, and it broke into several jagged pieces.

Payne was leaning against the doorway looking out, satisfied with the day when he overheard two men talking outside the next home. He didn't move.

"A murder! A good soldier murdered! I trust the general will get to the bottom of this. But I must say, I am glad these savages are finally gone. A sigh of relief, to be sure," said one.

"Yes, thank God," said the other.

– 14 –

Tricked

The boys nearly tripped over each other trying to get into the hideaway first that afternoon. Both wanted to get as far away as they could from that morning's events at church. When they got inside, Callie was sitting on her usual tree stump. She glanced up at them. Her exhaustion from not having slept well since the night the soldiers came was clearing.

She had just woken up, and her hair had tumbled out of its two thick braids during the night. She was re-braiding it, her long, graceful fingers moving smoothly and efficiently weaving her straight, black hair into what looked like intertwined ribbons. When she was done and had tied the ends with a thin piece of leather, she took a deep breath and looked up. She had been in her own world, and both boys stood quietly until she was finished.

"Holy Moses! You're really here! It seems like you're here, then you're going somewhere, then you're not. Shucks, I just don't know anymore!" said George. He moved toward her and gave her an awkward hug when she stood to greet him.

"Hello, George, hello!" she said, putting her arms around his small, bony shoulders. "Food, please?" She was staring at the picnic basket Jameson was holding.

He removed the red-and-white checkered cloth from the top of his lunch basket. She peeked inside, and Jameson set it on top of one of the tree stumps. She stood as she ate. There was a large piece of bread she shared with the boys. Between bites of apple and dried beef, she smiled at the boys with her slightly crooked teeth.

"What happened? Will you tell me now? Jameson said you should tell your own story," said George.

Callie's mind flooded with images and sounds. She sat down, and George and Jameson each took a seat on a stump. Jameson picked up his coat from the ground and put it on; it was still warm from Callie's body heat. She wanted to tell George what happened to her village but had no desire to go through the entire story again. George could not know about the murder, though. She wasn't sure she would catch up to her family now. It was time to make new plans, and her head was spinning.

George was so sincere that she decided to talk a little about the night. After describing some of the events, she said, "I did not know what to do. I could not move or help. My people are on a long trail and will not come back. That man who hurt King-er, he had Blossom on his saddle."

George's eyes widened. "Lula's little sister, right? Is she all right?"

"No, I'm sorry. She fell off his saddle and is dead. He did not care. I covered her in the woods with my bearskin blanket."

"This is the most terrible thing I ever heard. I'm cold," George said as he picked up the blanket Callie had been sleeping on. She saw his hands shaking.

"I hate that man. I truly hate him," said Jameson, and he kicked at the floor a few times with his well-worn boot. He remembered he had told George that he and Callie went to the saloon to get Big Dog, but Callie didn't know he had told George. He was losing track of his secrets and lies and felt a little dizzy. "Last night she tried to get Big Dog at the saloon to go after her family, but it didn't work out," Jameson said to George.

Callie looked at him anxiously. "Have you told your father?" she asked Jameson.

"What? What are you telling your pa? Is this the secret?" George asked, turning to look at Jameson.

"Nothin'. Nothin'. I don't know what you mean," Jameson said. He looked sternly at Callie.

The three of them sat in silence for a short time. Jameson put his hands around his forehead as if his head hurt. George was quiet but looked back and forth between Jameson and Callie as if he needed some answers, she thought.

"Callie, this morning was church. Many people were there, and they were talking about Rattlesnake Springs. They were talking about what happened," Jameson said.

She breathed faster, fear and anger rising again. Carefully choosing his words, Jameson continued. "And General Scott announced a soldier had been murdered, and they are looking for the man who did it," he said.

"The whole world is falling apart, right here in Tennessee! So many problems!" said George.

Callie stared at Jameson. Where was this conversation going, she wondered? She got off her stump and picked up her blue shawl from the ground near her bedding, draping it across her shoulders.

"And some people...many people walked to your village," he said.

"Why?" she asked, her head muddled by everything coming at her.

He couldn't get the words out right away. "Because . . . because they went through each house and took things they wanted."

"No, no!" she said and sat down hard.

George looked down at his feet. "I can't believe it. But it's true. My parents and Jameson's ma and pa didn't go. But the sure fact is that many did," he said, his voice trailing off.

Callie had forgotten about her necklace in the chaos of

the last few days but thought it would still be safe in its bowl. It was small, and maybe no one had seen it. More images flooded her as she pictured one thing after another being stolen. "Little Wolf's toy! People would not take his top! Ama's herb baskets for health and for sacred spirits, they didn't take these! Waya's peace pipes, oh no. He worked so hard to have peace with the soldiers." Her voice became quieter and her breathing shallower. "They did take things. I know now. The evil *U-ya* came again. Bad people took everything. My family, my life, everything is gone."

George walked over to her. Tears trickled down his face, and he sat on the ground near the stump she was sitting on. He looked up into her brown eyes brimming with tears but didn't speak. Jameson sat silently on his stump, and Callie relaxed a little when she saw how much her friends cared for her. She unclenched her hands and smoothed out her shawl.

Finally, George stood and picked up the purple marbles' basket Callie had made for him. He rolled some of his precious marbles around in one hand, got down on his knees in playing position, and looked up. "I don't know what to do, but please, let's play," he said to them.

Jameson joined him on the ground. Callie followed. They played marbles late into the afternoon. But there was no energy, none of the usual laughing and cheering. There was no delight.

While they were playing, King showed up to fetch George home for supper. His short, happy barks brought some liveliness back into the hideaway. Callie smiled. "King-er!" she said.

"Here, boy," George said as King bounded over to him. He buried his entire hand into the dog's furry back and gave him lots of good pats. "Ma wants me to come home for supper. No bath tonight! I'll walk along the river. Do you want to go with me? I'll show you my new slingshot. Ma got a bunch of them in the last store shipment, and I got to pick out the one I wanted first!"

This news piqued Jameson's interest. "Where is it? I don't see it," he said. This was a prized toy. Callie tilted her head, curious.

"What is this slingshot thing?" she asked.

George grinned and reached under his green-and-blue plaid, cotton-filled coat. He had stuffed it into the back of his gray wool pants, which Jameson noticed were getting shorter by the day as he got taller. "Right here!" he said as he pulled it out of his rope belt. "Right here!"

George hesitated when Jameson reached for it. "Be careful. Be real careful. But I guess you can hold it," he said. Callie laughed.

Jameson took it reverently from George and turned it all around, studying how it worked. There were two sturdy leather straps, each about two feet long. They were open on one end, and on the other end a small leather pouch held the straps together. Braided leather around the edges of the pouch gave it shape and stability. Jameson was examining how the pouch's two straps connected when George got nervous.

"Give it back. You can't do that," he said.

"You don't have to get all upset. I ain't gonna eat it!"

Callie laughed. "You are funny. It's not food!" She noticed Jameson's cheeks were turning pink.

"Let's go, and I'll show you how it works!" said George.

They all wanted to be free of the tension of the earlier conversation and walked lazily to the Hiawassee River and sat on the bank. Crickets, birds, and frogs sang their afternoon songs. The sun was setting and it shone on the swiftly moving water, breaking the surface into sparkly fragments. They passed the slingshot among the three of them.

George stood and searched the ground intently as if looking for something. He found a good-sized rock, and shouted,

"Got it!" He took his stance and put his right foot quite far out in front of his left.

"Don't fall over!" Jameson laughed.

Callie watched his movements intently. George ignored his friend and held both slingshot straps in his right hand. He struggled to get the rock firmly into the pouch, and it kept falling to the ground. This did not deter him, and he patiently picked it back up. After several attempts, he got it stabilized in the pouch, told Callie and Jameson to stand back while he swung the contraption around his head in big circles. He let go of one strap while holding tightly onto the other. The rock sputtered out of the pocket a few feet in front of him.

"It takes practice. I'm just a startin'," he said. Callie noticed his cheeks were also pink.

"Let me try. Come on, can I try?" Jameson said.

"Here. But it's not easy. You have to practice. You're supposed to aim for something. Like a tree or something," said George.

Callie was alternately watching the boys and the twinkling river. The peaceful river gave life to the Cherokee. It was sacred with its generous gifts of water and fish. The swirling, dangerous currents hypnotized her, and a heavy sadness washed over when she thought of the people who tried to escape in the river only days ago. When Jameson spoke, she snapped out of her trance and watched him. The slingshot was a little different from what the Cherokee men used to hunt small game with but also familiar to her once she saw George's efforts.

"I'm gonna hit that tree over there! Watch me!" said Jameson. He lined up his shot, using even more exaggerated movements than George. He planted his feet exactly right and positioned his arms at the proper angle. His eyes darted back and forth between the spot on the tree and the empty slingshot pouch which he held out at arm's length. Callie smiled to herself and wondered why he always prepared so elaborately.

She didn't think it helped him.

After he found the right rock, he worked for several minutes at getting his stance down. Callie saw him walk in small circles, picking up one stone, dropping it, and discovering another. When he found the perfect rock, bigger than George's, he let out a whoop.

With more grace than George, he placed the stone sturdily in the pouch, took his practiced stance, set his eyes on the trunk of a large tree thirty feet away, and swung the rock overhead several times. When he let go of one strap, the rock flew. It hit the tree on its far edge, nearly missing it. King ran to the tree and picked up the stone. Halfway back to Jameson, the dog lost interest and dropped it.

"Gosh! I did it! I did it! This is sure enough the greatest toy ever!" he said. Callie went and picked up his rock while King bounced around her legs. She walked back to Jameson and held out her hand. George nodded yes and Jameson handed her the slingshot.

"My turn," she said. "There, on the river." She pointed to a spot that was twice as far away as the tree.

Jameson gave George a slight smile and nod of his head. "She can't do it," he whispered. Callie heard it, and George ignored him.

"Go! You can do it! Go!" said George.

She got into her natural position for throwing things. The rock dropped to the ground once as she tried to place it in the pouch, but the second time it nestled in perfectly. She swung the rock around her head in larger, looser circles than the boys had done. When she let go of a strap, her arm followed through as the rock arched into the air and landed exactly where she had pointed. A loud splash followed.

"I win! I win, King-er!" she said, doing her game dance, right foot kicking backward, red moccasin beads clicking while she moved in tight circles. Both boys laughed and clapped. She slowed down after a bit but continued to twirl in wide, slow circles, dipping low and coming back up to full height in a dream-like dance.

"You're awful good at games, Callie. Shucks, I've got to go. Ma doesn't like supper to get cold if she has to wait for me," said George. A flock of geese heading south for warmer weather passed low overhead. King barked enthusiastically at their noisy honks.

"Well, I know some people even shoot birds with slingshots," said Jameson.

"I have no idea why I would shoot a bird with a rock. That bird has never done nothin' to me. Why would I want to hurt her?" said George.

Callie's dancing stopped. Her smile melted away. "I did nothing to the soldiers. My people did no harm. Why do they want to hurt us?" she said, staring again at the wide Hiawassee.

"I'm sure sorry all of this has happened to you and your family. I . . . I," said George, nervously tugging at his left suspender, slingshot hanging from his right hand. "I wish your people and our people could be friends. We don't need your land, and it's terrible unfair to take it. Ma and pa say that if we can't stop evil, we can at least do something good." He paused. "Maybe this will help you feel strong." He held out his slingshot to her.

"Oh, George!" she said, taking it gently. "You are good. We can all share it and then we are strong together."

George and King went home while Jameson and Callie headed back to the hideaway. It felt to Callie as if for a few hours that afternoon, things had been normal. The sun would set and tomorrow it would rise. One step followed another. This was how her people thought about the world and what Waya had taught her. Yet, her world had tumbled recently, and Callie knew there was no predictability. What was her next step?

Catching up to her family seemed impossible now, and she desperately wanted some kind of plan.

Once inside the hideaway, they sat on their tree stumps and, through the open door, watched the sky turn orange and pink as the sun set. It was a lovely scene, but good things don't always last, she thought. Tomorrow might be ugly. The beautiful river had tricked her today. For a short time, it had made things seem tranquil, peaceful.

But things were not.

John Payne was larger than Callie realized. Jameson had lit the candle moments before Payne entered, and the man's shadow bounced off the walls of the hideaway. Payne swayed as he tried to close the branch-and-twine door behind him, but it remained part way open. For a moment, Callie thought she and Jameson could rush at him, knock him over, and escape, but the knife he was waving looked deadly. Callie and Jameson stood and then backed away, bumping into the wall behind them. They had been so engrossed in thought, they didn't hear him arrive.

Payne had a long piece of thick rope looped around his shoulder. "Sit! Sit down, I said," were his first words. Big Dog stood outside the hideaway, tied to a large branch on the oak tree. Through the open door, Callie saw she was skittish as she tossed her freckled head this way and that, pawing at the ground.

Callie and Jameson each sat down on one of the tree stump chairs about three feet apart. Jameson looked shocked and pale, and Callie noticed his hands were shaking.

"What, what do you want? What are you going to do to us?" Jameson asked. His voice cracked.

"Shut up, you little brat," Payne said. He spoke quietly and slurred his words.

Payne lurched toward them, and Callie felt nauseous when she smelled the alcohol that seemed to come out of not only his mouth but every part of his body. His dark blue military coat was open, and he was so close she could see that a button in the middle of the coat was missing.

"Move those stumps together. Now," he said.

It occurred to Callie she could scream for help, and she glanced at Jameson. He turned his head slightly to look at her too. She opened her mouth, trying to give him a signal. He seemed to understand her thought but shook his head just a bit, left then right. Callie realized no one could hear them this far away from both the fort and Rattlesnake Springs. She moved her stump next to Jameson's and sat back down.

Payne was clumsy, but he was strong. In one quick motion, he put his knife on the ground out of reach for Callie and Jameson. As Jameson's eyes followed it, Payne shoved Jameson's shoulder toward Callie so forcefully that she almost fell off the stump.

She looked at Payne sternly. "You stole Shiko Waka, and Mohe is dead. You are a mean man."

He shifted his eyes to her, raised his hand, and slapped her. She recoiled but quickly sat back up.

"It's about time I did that to you. You're just a dirty little Injun girl. You act like you're so high and mighty."

Callie began to stand and lifted her right hand to strike Payne, but Jameson pulled her back down to the stump. His eyes met Payne's. "You can't hit her."

"Watch me." Payne slapped Callie again. This time she fell off the stump but slowly got back on with as much dignity as she could. Payne took his rope and tied it around Jameson's shoulders and pulled it tight. "Shut your face up, boy. Why are you trying to protect her? You're white, and your father is a soldier. It makes you filthy to even be near Injuns. She's your little girlfriend. Huh? Is that right?"

Jameson said nothing. Payne stumbled backward a step while he awkwardly but surely added Callie into the coarse rope he had tied around Jameson. Both Callie and Jameson were now tied together around their shoulders, chest, upper arms, and forearms with a knot in back.

Payne picked up his knife and put it back in the leather sheath at his waist. As he sat down and faced them, his stump rocked a little. He pulled out a small bottle of whiskey from his coat pocket and unscrewed the cap. After finishing the bottle, he tossed it aside and sat looking at them for what seemed like a long time to Callie.

"Look-ee what we have here, all tied up nice. How 'bout we have a little talk? Let's start with what you both saw at the saloon last night, shall we?" he began.

– 15 –

Distractions

"We didn't see anything. We didn't see anything at all. Please let us go," said Jameson.

Payne ignored him. He stared at Callie. "Oh, I think you both saw something. I saw that Injun girl look right at me."

"Yes, I saw. I saw you hurt the soldier's neck. I saw," she said clearly.

"An honest squaw! What do ya know about that? Yeah, I killed that worthless fool. He had taken my poker money one too many times. No one is going to miss him. And no one is going to find out who did it. Do you hear me, you little brats?"

"Yes, yes. We do, and we didn't see anything. Right, Callie, right?" said Jameson.

Callie, whose head was almost touching Jameson's as they sat tied together, turned toward him slightly and then back to face Payne. "I saw," she said.

Payne stood and let out a hoot, "Whooey! You don't know what you're in for, brave girl! What's your name? Oh, wait, I know, Callie."

Callie stiffened. Payne continued. "You know how I know that? Huh? Maybe you remember this?" He reached into his jacket pocket and pulled out Dove's necklace, swinging it back and forth in front of her.

Callie stared at it, confused. Her orange beaded necklace

was supposed to be in its clay bowl by her sleeping mat. With the turmoil of the last few days, she had forgotten about it.

"Where you get this?" she asked, carefully controlling her voice.

"It was in your hut. You savages deserve nothing, but I'll tell you what, we all got plenty. But how did I know it was *your* hut? Let's think . . . Oh, I remember now. Want to know, Ca-llie?" Payne said.

Jameson threw himself against the rope. "Not everyone took things! You're a no-good, but some white people respect the Cher—" Callie looked at Jameson and nodded in quiet agreement.

Payne, who had forgotten about Jameson, glanced at him and snapped, "Shut your mouth."

Callie felt her anger change to fear and didn't know what was about to come. She raised her head and saw the *U-ya*, bright as day, hiding deep inside Payne's eyes.

Payne began. "Here we go! How about a bedtime story for you kids? One night about fifteen years ago, right after they sent me to this hellhole of a fort, I took myself an evening walk, a little stroll, shall we say. Rattlesnake Springs looked interesting. Sure was. The first hut I came to turned out to be yours. I invited myself in, I sure did. Your mother was alone inside, and oh, she looked pretty."

Jameson was staring at the ground, and Callie felt his arm muscle tighten. She continued to stare straight at the *U-ya*.

"Now, this necklace caught my eye." He held it up again and moved closer to the lamp. "See? See?"

Payne turned around and suddenly threw the necklace out the door. Birds flew from their perches in the trees into the safety of the sky, startled. Callie watched as the lightweight necklace seemed to float in slow motion as it left his hands. He shoved the door shut, turned back to Callie and Jameson, and stood, towering over them.

"Your mother was stronger than I expected, and that

necklace was still on her pretty little neck when I left. And I imagine it's yours now."

Jameson felt vomit rise in his mouth. Callie sat still as if she had turned to stone or had magically become an extension of the wooden stump she was sitting on. All she could think to do was to keep staring down the *U-ya* behind Payne's eyes.

He went on. "You people are just plain dumb. Your mother, what was her name? Yeah, Dove. I heard she gave you the name—Callie. Couldn't even pronounce it right. She named you after her white teacher friend, Katherine. There was an Injun lover if there ever was one. Your mother was trying to name you Kathie and like the rest of you worthless savages, she could not even say English right. See what I'm sayin', Kathie, Callie? Hey, Callie? Talk to your daddy." He drunkenly rocked back on his heels and then steadied himself on the wall.

A shock wave slammed into Callie's head. Her jaws clenched tight. She tried to process this, but time had become compressed, dense. She felt trapped. What he was saying seemed unrelated to her. She knew she had light skin for a Cherokee girl, but there were many shades of skin color in her tribe. It was not out of the ordinary.

"I hate you. Dove hate you. Cherokee people hate you."

"Why! That's no way to talk to your father! Maybe you need another slapping!" he said and spat on the ground as he swayed a little.

"Her name means Dove, but her Cherokee name is Woya. She was strong and kind. Good. Good woman."

"Who cares? Wo-ya, Woy-a. Now your little family is gone for good. Gone! And you, all alone, poor Callie. Ha! I can sure tell you that nobody white is cryin' over that!" he said.

"Not true! There are nice white people. Jameson and George are good." She and Jameson looked at each other, and they felt bravery take hold.

"I never, never say your name. Your name is dead. You

hurt my mother. You steal my people. But you do not take me," Callie said as her head began to clear.

Payne sat down and put both elbows on his knees, resting his head in his hands. "Now, now, enough of our friendly chatter. Let's get down to the real business. What to do? What to do with a couple of worthless kids? You saw me kill that soldier, but he deserved it! Your tiny brains won't ever understand that. But you sure as hell won't tell nobody about that night."

This time Jameson said nothing in defense. Fright was leaving him, and he was thinking about escaping. He had no specific plan, but an energy had sparked inside him.

Payne continued. "But wait, you two understand how dangerous the Hiawassee River is. Yeah, you might have just been two sinful teenagers who went for a lovebird walk tonight, but you got too close to that big, ol' river. Shame on you! White boy, Injun girl. Shame, shame. Nobody will take much pity on you." He paused, pleased with himself. "It'll take awhile to find your bodies, won't it? The river sure is cold this time of year, and that current never stops. Never."

A noise outside distracted Callie. She thought she heard King in the bushes. He barked and scratched at the closed hideaway door.

"What the—" Payne stood and clumsily opened the door. King tried to go inside, but Payne blocked him with his foot. "Get, get away, you dumb mutt!" said Payne, kicking at him. King moved but kept barking.

As Payne went outside to quiet the dog by any means necessary, Callie's free hand reached into the leather pouch hanging at her side. While Payne had been tying her and Jameson together, she had positioned the pouch so she could get at it. Although her arms were tied, her right hand was free. She carefully pulled out her knife, struggled to get it under the looped rope around Jameson's forearm and, in one clean stroke, sliced through it. The poorly tied rope untangled easily. Once his arms were free, Jameson took the knife and helped Callie get loose. They were quiet and efficient. Outside, Payne was chasing King, both running in circles near the horse, but the dog easily outpaced the drunken man.

Jameson went to the game corner of the hideaway and picked up the solid bat branch, four inches in diameter, and got into position as if he were playing with George. Jameson was ready to hit a heavy rock off a tree stump as far and as hard as he could, ready to impress his good pal. Callie nodded her head at him.

She peeked out the open door and saw the horse and dog getting more frantic. Big Dog yanked wildly at the old, frayed rope keeping her tied to the tree, swinging her head back and forth trying to break away. She was whinnying loudly, nostrils flaring. King snarled and pulled back his lips as he showed Payne his teeth. Unable to catch him, Payne stopped but yelled, "Shut up! Shut up!" while waving his hands in the air to scare away the anxious dog. It spooked Big Dog even more. The dog surged forward to snap at the unstable man's legs and then backed up as Payne lunged at him. Forward and back. Payne stood with his back to Callie and Jameson, swatting King away from his legs.

Callie wanted to kill Payne. She wanted to kill the man who had taken so much from her. Standing inside the door, she raised her seven-inch knife. Her eyes were dead center in the middle of Payne's back. She knew a knife in the back could kill a man. Jameson had stepped out of the hideaway and was standing just outside the door. He gripped the branch with both hands as if ready to strike some invisible thing, staring at Callie. With a snap of her wrist, she let go of the knife and watched it fly toward Payne, but at the last second, she had changed her mind and shifted her aim from his back to his right shoulder. She would not become like him, a murderer.

He stumbled forward and let out a long howl. He recovered his balance, swung around, and walked straight toward

Callie, thirty feet away. The knife had lodged in his shoulder. King continued to snarl and dive at Payne's legs. Big Dog jerked hard, and the rope finally snapped. She was free.

Payne was only twenty feet from Callie when Jameson quickly moved toward him and said, "I saw you too."

As Payne turned to look, Jameson swung the branch with all his might. He hit him square in the chest. The branch broke in two. Payne lost his balance and flew backward onto the ground with a stunned look on his face.

Big Dog, who was near Payne when he fell, was startled. Her neighing became louder and higher pitched. Foam dripped from her mouth. The horse began to rear. Her front legs leaped high off the ground and then came crashing back down. Twelve hundred pounds. Over and over. Again and again. And under those powerful legs was John Payne.

– 16 –

Gone

Thomas and William burst through the scruffy undergrowth into the clearing. George followed close behind his father. King, who had been standing next to the tree, ran to George's side. The nearly full moon illuminated the clearing, and the crisp air made the scene look brittle like it had been populated with still, glass figures that might shatter at any moment.

William moved toward Big Dog, who had finally stopped thrusting her front legs toward the sky. She was breathing heavily, and her broad back was dark with sweat. William murmured, "Easy, easy, girl." He petted her neck, veins bulging, in long comforting strokes while reaching for the frayed rope that hung loosely around her thick neck.

William looked down at the man lying on the ground, face up, while Thomas had immediately walked over to Jameson. "Are you all right, son?" Jameson had no voice but nodded his head. Thomas looked over at Callie, who saw his look of confusion and surprise at seeing her. She also nodded. He walked over to the body, bent down on one leg, and put two fingers on Payne's neck, looking for a pulse. Callie didn't understand what was happening and watched Thomas closely, worried that the *U-ya* might sit up and strangle him.

"He's dead. Why, it's John Payne!" said Thomas. He took a deep breath in and let it out slowly with a whoosh sound.

"What . . . what in the world happened?" asked William.

George, with King glued to his side, walked over to his father who was still calming the agitated horse. George looked at Callie and Jameson and said, "I didn't tell pa. I didn't break our secret, Jameson! Please don't be mad at me. I didn't say what the secret was because I don't even know it. I just said you had a secret!"

Jameson's tight jaw loosened a bit, "Well, that is sort of still telling my secret. But it's fine. It's good you told your pa."

George let out a relieved sigh and continued. "I knew something was wrong. You and Callie had gone to the High Hopes Saloon twice; that ain't normal. No one even knew Callie was here. And it was time our folks knew about the hideaway. And you said 'real bad' about your secret. And now this rotten egg is dead! Something sure enough was going on!" he said proudly and snapped his blue suspenders.

Callie had not moved, nor had Jameson. They stood next to each other like thin, straight trees, trying to blend into the woods.

"I think for now the most important thing is that everyone is safe. No one is hurt," said Thomas.

"Pa, I'm sorry I didn't tell you all this. I don't know why. I'm glad you are here, so glad," said Jameson.

Thomas smiled and said, "I'm right here, son." He continued, "We'll sort this out tomorrow. It's time to go home. Enough for tonight."

Callie snapped out of her trance and walked over to the horse. She stroked her nose. "Her name is Shiko Waka. She is a good horse, and he was an evil man. The *U-ya* was in him. He stole her from Mohe. Then, he killed a soldier at the saloon."

Thomas turned to her, "John Payne is his name. I sure don't understand things, but mostly I don't know how you are here, Callie. I couldn't be happier to see you."

Callie didn't know what came over her, but she hurried over to Thomas and hugged him around the waist. He pulled back a bit in surprise and then put his arms around her. When she released the hug, he showed her what he was holding in his hand. "I found this on the ground. Is it yours?" he said.

She took her necklace from him and put it on. She patted it, looked down at it, and said, "Woya." When she moved back to Jameson's side, she found herself warmer, safer. She needed her necklace and Dove's strength to bolster her. He nodded approvingly at her.

"Callie, I want you to hold the horse's rope." began Thomas.

When George shouted, "Big Dog's a hero!" some tension in the clearing released, moved somewhere else, into the earth or into the air. Callie saw everyone smile, a little letting go.

Thomas laughed. "She might be. William, let's lift this man onto the horse."

Working together, they laid Payne face down across the horse's strong back, behind the saddle. The horse stood oddly still for the process, staring at Callie as she petted the mare's nose. Callie handed the rope to Thomas, and while they were busy organizing the horse and its load, she quietly picked up her knife, which had dislodged from Payne's shoulder when he fell. After wiping it on the short, dry prairie grass, she put it back in her pouch.

"Let's go home," said Thomas. The group moved with Thomas at the head of the line, leading the horse and its cargo. William walked beside Big Dog with his hand ready to steady the body if needed. George and King followed. The dog ran in and out of the brush, sniffing out rabbits. Jameson and Callie were last and talked in hushed tones with each other.

"I don't know what to say. I . . . I . . . he is your father. You must be so angry," said Jameson, staring straight ahead.

"I do not care about him, but I know this one thing," she said. "I know he is evil, and evil is not in my family."

"You are the strongest person I know. You and your Cherokee people have suffered, but I can see their strength in you. I'm sorry your family is gone. I'm sorry your plan didn't work out. I'm just sorry for everything," he said.

"It is true, my plan did not work. You try to help. Thank you," she said. "My mother told me when life does not work right, we must walk on."

Jameson stopped and faced her. He opened his arms, and she stepped into them. Tears flooded her eyes. Sometimes she wasn't sure if she was strong. She needed other people to show her the way, but her family was gone. As he hugged her and felt her sleek hair, smooth on his cheek, he whispered, "I'm proud to be your friend."

Her eyes couldn't hold the sorrow. They stood, Jameson holding her tight, while her body shook with sobs.

When the group neared the fort, William, George, and King headed home. Thomas told Callie and Jameson to go inside the house and get warm. He led Big Dog around the outside walls of the fort, all the way back to the loading docks. He stopped when he found a stack of empty gunny sacks piled in a corner. The docks were huge. At least ten wagons could line up in front of them to be unloaded and emptied of their treasures, mostly food and supplies. But as bustling as it was in the day, it was deadly quiet at night.

He gently pushed Payne off the still horse and tried to let him fall onto the gunny sacks with a little dignity, a kindness Payne had never shown people or animals. Instead, Payne dropped onto the rough gunny sacks with a thud, just as his own horse had dropped to the prairie when he shot her days earlier and just as Mohe had. Thomas stood for a moment staring down at him and then led Big Dog away. He put her with the other horses in the fort's corral and went home.

Jameson and Callie had waited outside on the small porch. Jameson hadn't gone inside because he didn't know what to say to his mother and needed his father's guidance.

Thomas walked up the stairs and put his arm around his son's shoulders. "Let's get warmed up," he said.

Katherine ran to the door. "Oh, my Lord! I've been so worried! What happened? You all look like you're going to collapse right here on the floor!" They walked into the kitchen, and she pulled out three chairs from the wooden table, motioning for them to sit.

"Now, Kathie," Thomas began. Upon hearing the name Kathie, Callie's heart skipped a beat. "We'll tend to the story tomorrow. They're fine, you can see that. Just fine."

Katherine filled the teapot with well water that was sitting in a large bucket next to the stove. She opened the grate and stuffed another piece of wood into the black potbellied stove. The kitchen warmed up, and the water was soon ready for the tea leaves. She poured the hot tea into mugs and sat down.

"The first order of business is to welcome Callie! My goodness, I don't know how or where you came from, but oh, honey...," Katherine said and walked behind Callie's chair to kiss her on the top of her head. This kind of kiss was familiar to Callie. Both her grandmother and mother were affectionate. But little else seemed normal to her. She had never been in a white person's home.

She knew about tea. Her family often drank a kind of tea. Honey locust trees had big pods that released their flavor in boiling water, but when she took a sip of the tea in front of her, she wanted to spit it out. She swallowed, knowing it was the polite thing to do but struggled with the rest of the cup of bitter black tea. She sat stiff in the odd chair as Thomas, Katherine, and Jameson babbled away. They spoke too quickly for her to understand everything. She didn't want to understand. She didn't want to think.

When everyone had finished their tea and Callie's cup was half empty, Thomas said, "All right now. It's time for sleep."

Katherine left the table and disappeared into a room to

the left of the kitchen. Callie could hear noises coming from the room like things were being moved around. She came back to the kitchen shortly.

"Callie, this will be your room tonight. Please come with me."

Callie followed Katherine into a small, white-painted room. There was one window, which was covered with a large piece of bright yellow fabric, a curtain. She saw many other pieces of colored cloth thrown together in the corner of the room. There was a large wooden cupboard with its doors closed. She was both curious and a little frightened about what was inside.

Katherine saw her staring and said, "This is just a wardrobe." She walked over and began to open the two doors. Callie jumped back and tumbled onto the narrow bed behind her. Katherine stopped immediately.

"Let's not think about that now. You found your bed!" Katherine sat on the edge of the bed with Callie, who was trying to figure out how to sit on it. It was too soft. Callie couldn't get comfortable so she stood up. Katherine lay down on it and pulled the pillow under her head.

"Like this, lie like this, and then you'll go to sleep." The wood in the potbellied stove in the kitchen made a low cackling noise as it burned. There were muffled sounds coming from the kitchen as the others continued to talk.

Callie had seen beds, but not many, in some wealthy Cherokee homes. Even so, why did it have to be so high off the ground? Where was the bottom of it? Would she just fall into a hole in the middle? And what was this thing that sat under your head, she wondered.

Katherine stood, and Callie lay down on her back, straight as a board with the pillow under her neck instead of cushioning her head. She turned her head to keep an eye on the wardrobe. Katherine smiled, went over to the large wooden closet and gently opened the doors. Callie saw one of Katherine's shawls and a few other clothing items along with some kind of string and small, round pieces of wood covered with fabric.

She got up and picked up one of the round items. Her curiosity trumped fear. She turned it over and over trying to figure out its purpose.

Katherine laughed and said, "That's to embroider with. We can do it together and maybe sew a pretty flower." Callie said nothing and went back to her stiff sitting position on the bed.

"Thank you, Mrs. Miller," Callie said quietly. Shyness was not a typical response for her, but everything was so different. Katherine bent to take off her moccasins as she sat rigid on the bed.

"No," Callie said. She wanted nothing more to disrupt her. The moccasins were fine on her feet. They were familiar, hers, when nothing else seemed to be.

Katherine picked up a heavy patchwork quilt, folded neatly on a chair by the wardrobe. Callie realized that the same pieces of cloth in the pile had somehow made their way onto the quilt. Katherine gently laid the quilt over her after she had laid down. Callie, still nervous about moving too much on the bed, shifted only her eyes to murmur, "Thank you."

"Good night, dear," Katherine stepped out and softly closed the door.

Callie pulled the quilt up around her shoulders. It wasn't a bearskin, but it was warm and thick. She turned on her side to get comfortable, but something was wrong. When she realized it was the pillow, she pushed it to the floor and instantly fell asleep.

"I guess I pretty much saved everyone! Don't you think, Jameson? I wish I was there for the whole gosh darn adventure at the hideaway last night, but it was all done when I got there. I never get to have the real fun," said George, as his voice went from squeaky excitement to disappointment. "What happened anyway?"

Jameson's and George's families, along with Callie, sat on Katherine's extra kitchen chairs, squeezed around the small rectangular wooden table the next morning. Everyone had a cup of tea sitting before them, but Callie was hesitant to drink it after last night's introduction to the sharp-tasting liquid. She took a tiny sip now and then as they talked.

"I should start by telling you, Ma and Pa, that I am sorry. I lied to you. Twice. I said I was going to George's house, but I was trying to help Callie," said Jameson.

George's mother looked sternly at him, but George kept looking straight ahead. Callie noticed the tension and said, "Yes, George and Jameson help me. When the soldiers came to Rattlesnake Springs, I was in the woods. They take all my people, all my family. But I was left behind. That man, that soldier, John Payne, had my little friend, Blossom, on his horse and dropped her. He didn't care, and she is dead."

"Oh, I'm so sorry. I can't imagine," said Katherine quietly, shaking her head.

Callie paused. "I stay at the hideaway in the woods. I want to see Shiko Waka, Mohe's horse that bad man stole. I ask Jameson to take me into town to see her at the saloon where the man was playing cards."

"That was the first time I lied, Ma." She glanced at him and raised her eyebrows.

"But I had a better idea. I ask Jameson to take me to the saloon the next night and I would get Shiko Waka and ride her through the night and catch my family. But this did not happen. We went to the saloon, but we saw a terrible thing."

"We saw John Payne rob and then murder a soldier. We saw it all. And he saw us. He threatened me at church," said Jameson.

"Why didn't you come to me immediately?" asked Thomas.

"I know I should have. Callie told me to," Jameson said.

Thomas smiled at Callie.

"Did you not tell him?" she asked and backed away from

the table in frustration.

"I was going to. I swear. I wanted to wait just one day. Ma and pa didn't know you were at the hideaway, and General Scott announced in church he'd find the man. I just needed one day. It all happened so fast. I'm sorry. I truly am," said Jameson.

"Go on, please. And let's be thankful no one is hurt," said Katherine.

"Someone is hurt. The last time I saw him, John Payne was lying dead on a pile of gunny sacks at the loading dock. I'll be leaving soon to talk with General Scott," said Thomas.

"What? What has been going on?" said Katherine.

Callie took a deep breath. "I—"

Before she could say more, George interrupted. "I didn't tell pa the secret last night. I just said you *had* a secret, a real bad one. Then, my pa went to see your pa, and they told me to take them to the hideaway. Anyway, I have been wanting them to see it. It sure is fine. Don't you think, Pa?"

William and then Thomas said it was fine indeed, and that George did the right thing. George glanced at his mother, who looked at him sternly but with kind eyes. She asked Callie to continue.

"Jameson and I were in the hideaway yesterday afternoon. I sleep there. And thank you for the very good bread and stew, Mrs. Miller!"

Katherine suddenly understood that the food had gone to Callie, not Mary, and smiled.

"The bad man came to the hideaway. He say he know we saw him kill the soldier. He say he will drown us, and it will look like an accident," she said.

"Dear Lord. I will pray in gratitude for the rest of my life that you are safe," said Katherine.

Callie looked around the table. All eyes were on her. She tugged at her braids. "He tie us up, but he was heavy with alcohol. Shiko Waka was wild, so much noise and anger. King-er came, and she is more wild. I cut the rope around us when the man tells the animals to be quiet. I throw my knife into his shoulder. Jameson, with a very strong stick, hit him in the chest, and he fell. Shiko Waka was free of her rope, and she stepped high on him. Many times."

"I see. I understand now. You did things right. That was good thinking, son," Thomas said. Jameson grinned.

"Dang!" said George. "That was sure enough bad. King gets a treat tonight! A big ol' bone. He's a hero, kind of!"

"We will go back to the hideaway. And King-er too." Callie paused. "But not for some little time. The bad things there must fly away, and then it will be good again." She saw everyone smile warmly at her, nodding their heads in agreement. Katherine reached out to touch her hand, but Callie pulled it back. Things were going too fast. She needed to think.

The adults began to talk all at once, but Callie interrupted them. She didn't know how it would come out but said what was simple and true, the way her uncle taught her to speak. "There is something more. Something that is hard to say. That U-ya man said he is my father, but I know Dove hated him. I hate him too. He told me about my name."

Silence settled around the table. "He say my mother named me after you, Mrs. Miller, because you are friends. After your name Kathie, but we say it a little different in Cherokee. So, it is Callie."

Katherine stood and gently pulled Callie to stand. Katherine hugged her with every ounce of reassurance and kindness in her. She kissed her forehead and gently rocked her back and forth as they stood. The energy changed in the room. Callie felt it; the U-ya was finally gone. Her body softened, and she let herself be cared for.

– 17 –

Careful

Thomas didn't know where this would end up. The less said the better, and he would need to navigate the conversation carefully. It was early the next morning, and he wanted to get this over with before the general got news of things.

"Thank you for seeing me on short notice, but it's a matter I think you'll be interested in, sir," Thomas said.

"What is it?" the general mumbled, mouth full of cigar. A cup of fragrant black coffee sat steaming in front of him.

"Last night, sir, a strange set of incidents came together, and—"

"And what?" snapped General Scott impatiently.

"I found out who murdered Sergeant Jones," said Thomas. He spoke boldly, but his heart was pounding.

"Unexpected news but, yes, good news, indeed!" said the general.

"My son, Jameson, you may remember him, told us he was going to his friend's house on the night of the murder. However, he went to the High Hopes Saloon—very much against our wishes, may I add."

"Why in the world would a young man go to a saloon?" asked the general, whose interest was now piqued. He laid the fat cigar in the dirty stone ashtray on his bulky, dark cherry wood desk and squinted at Thomas.

"Um, he's quite newly interested in the piano as it turns out. He knew there was a piano player there and wanted to hear him. I assure you, his lie is being dealt with."

The general was unusually silent and stared at Thomas.

"While he was there, he saw Sergeant Jones stumble out of the saloon, quite drunk, followed by none other than Second Lieutenant John Payne. My son saw Payne steal money from the man's pocket and strangle him. Payne saw Jameson too." Thomas kept right on going before the general could ask more questions.

"My son was in shock and didn't tell me about this. On Sunday night, Payne found Jameson playing at his hideaway in the woods and threatened to harm him. After a scuffle, Payne's horse, the one he took from that young Cherokee man ... sir ... the horse was highly agitated and crushed him to death."

"Ah ha! I am not surprised it was Payne. He's been a thorn in my side for years. Good riddance to him, I say. Where is the body?" asked the general.

"I put it by the loading docks. It is in the same spot you ordered us to put the dead Cherokee warrior."

"Good job! Yes, indeed. Now it's done," said the general, who picked up his cigar and took a long draw on it.

The general continued. "I received news early this morning about the Cherokee removal. It has been rather messy. My officers report wailing from the women and young people trying to run off the trail and escape into the woods. I ordered the officers not to shoot unless necessary."

He paused. "It appears it won't be necessary as already people are dropping dead, and it's only been a few days. No place or time to bury them, so the soldiers or their families move the bodies off the trail twenty or thirty feet and the others keep moving. People walking, dying, running, a disastrous operation. I wish I could have gotten more wagons from President Jackson, but this whole removal has been a hellish nightmare to organize. I hope you can appreciate my efforts, Thomas."

Thomas was silent. The general stood and paced behind his desk for a minute before sitting back down.

"We've been preparing all summer as you know. We set up forts along the way to give people rest as they walked west. But we're predicting that the damn problem is the disease that will spread like wildfire in these forts. Obviously, there's not enough food. And many drowned crossing rivers. I told my men to, at least, let them take off their shoes, ah, moccasins, to keep them dry before they go in the water, but I heard that roughneck Sergeant Holston wasn't allowing it. You can see I've tried, but how do you manage all of this? It's been a catastrophe." He took a drink of coffee but, as usual, didn't offer any to Thomas.

"We removed about thirteen thousand people, emptied Rattlesnake Springs and its surrounding villages, the last of sixteen thousand total. Of course, we want their farmland. They have taken good care of it. The land we moved them to is less fertile, and the hunting is poor. But! We paid them for some of their land, yes, we did. It wasn't a fair amount but let the record show that the government did purchase some Cherokee land. The record would also have to state that we did not always fulfill our agreement and pay, however."

He shuffled some paper on his desk. The general liked to talk, and it was Thomas's job to listen. "Yes, sir," said Thomas, looking at the general, but then shifting his gaze down.

After another sip of coffee, the general said more slowly, "It's colder than we thought, and the elderly and babies have little chance of making it. I didn't want people to die, Thomas. I really didn't, even though I knew they would. I ordered our officers to be moderate in their treatment, and I believe at least some have. No supplies, no solid plan. What did the president expect?" He paused. "So be it. I have fulfilled my job for the United States government to the best of my ability."

"Yes, sir. May I be excused?" asked Thomas. His head hurt, and he rubbed his temple.

The general nodded. "I'll take it from here. Do the explaining and such to my superiors on this whole John Payne mess." He brushed the little gold ropes hanging from his left shoulder, straightening them out.

Thomas stepped out into the early morning and stood looking at the cloudy October sky. He knew the general might see Callie around the fort but would likely take little notice of her. There were still a few Cherokee people here and there who had escaped into the hills. The wind had picked up, and it was a day to be inside, near the fire if possible. He was acutely aware that it was not something that was possible for thousands of innocent people. Leaning against the fort, he whispered a simple prayer for the Cherokee people. "Lord, hold them close and give them strength."

– 18 –

Later

Callie sat at the kitchen table, fiddling with her necklace. She had been with the Millers for three months, and it was an unusually cold January. That morning, she had helped Katherine make cornbread, using her mother and Ama's recipe. They would serve it later for Saturday afternoon tea, a tea she quite liked now. They often cooked together, teaching each other new ways birthed from old traditions. Several embroidered flower pictures hung on the walls of the kitchen.

They talked freely about Dove, but it surprised Callie when Katherine told her that Dove had confided in her that she was having a soldier's baby, a man she hated. She told Callie how honored she was that Dove named her daughter after her.

After her initial shock, Callie realized what a special friendship the two women had shared. She couldn't get enough of Katherine's memories of Dove. Callie never tired of one in particular.

"I watched your mother transform, truly bloom in her pregnancy with you. She would come to school and warm herself by the fire, listening closely to the English words. She caught on quickly like you do. I was slower at repeating the Cherokee words she taught me. I watched her fall in love with you over those nine months, cradling her belly, singing you sweet songs. She fell on the ice once in front of the school and was near crazy with worry. I gave her some tea, which she hated as much as you did the first time you tried it! And when you arrived in the world, I never saw a happier mother. I know you only had nine years with her before she died in childbirth with your little brother. It's not enough, but it's what you and she had. Those years will carry you through the rest of your life."

Callie's room was the same one she had slept in the first night she arrived. She had been going to school every day and her English was quickly improving, but verbs were still challenging. She taught some Cherokee words to the children in school, who giggled at each other's mispronunciations. To remember her language, she made up songs like the Bee Song and sang them to herself and to the schoolchildren. Callie and the boys decided they would go back to the hideaway in the spring. Even though there were bad memories, there were also good memories. Callie chose to think of the good ones.

Later that afternoon, Thomas walked in the front door, a little out of breath. He asked Jameson, Katherine, and Callie to join him at the kitchen table. As they sat down for tea, he laid a piece of paper on the table.

"I just had a meeting with Old Fuss and Feathers," Thomas said. Jameson looked at him, head tipped in curiosity. "I don't call him that to his face, of course, or around the soldiers." Jameson smiled at his father.

"Feathers? May-be he is like the chicken?" asked Callie. Laughter filled the room.

Thomas began, a little hesitantly. "I have some news to share of the Cherokee people's journey, if that's what it can be called," he said. He had been careful to pick out only certain facts from the *Chronicle* newspaper.

Callie felt the mood in the room shift. She had tried to move on in her new life until she could get back to her family. Grateful to be living with Katherine and all, she enjoyed going to school and had friends there. She anxiously pulled on her braid, tangling her fingers in its smoothness.

Thomas continued. "I know this is difficult, Callie. I'm sorry, but it's important to know some facts. I wish it were better news. The trail is now being called the Trail of Tears, and your people call it The Trail Where They Cried."

Callie looked down and whispered, "*Nunahi-Duna-Dlo-Hilu-I*, the trail where they cried."

Thomas continued. "There have been about sixteen thousand people total moved west, and about four thousand died, mostly of disease and exhaustion." Callie breathed in sharply. She expected deaths, but one in four seemed unbearable. The question she kept asking herself and had been asking since the day in the fields when she heard Ama and Waya talking was: Why? She knew about the taking of the land but how could the world be so unfair, so wounded? How would she find her way forward? She needed her family to guide her, but they were gone.

Thomas continued, "Several hundred people managed to escape and are setting up a new life in the hills around Rattlesnake Springs. The government is not going after them. The walk was about a thousand miles, and they are now trying to make it their home. Your people are strong, and I pray they will make a new life."

There was only silence. Callie nervously pulled on her braids. He picked up the piece of paper he had laid on the table. Thomas began again, even more tenderly this time. "I have a letter, too. It is from your Uncle Waya." Callie's brain clicked into gear and her breath came more quickly now.

"It's a privilege to read it to you. He sent it to the fort and to me specifically. But it's for you." Thomas took a deep breath in.

"*My Dear Callie,*
What trials we have been through! I am uncertain how you became separated from us on that darkest of days, but our grief at losing you was more difficult than the walk itself. I have asked, with the help of a few

good soldiers, about your well-being. I understand you are living with the school teacher, Mrs. Miller, and her family. I could not be happier. As you know, she and your mother were good friends. This was unusual for a Cherokee and a white woman to be so close, but it speaks well for the kind character of both women.

The Nunahi-Duna-Dlo-Hilu-I, The Trail Where They Cried, has produced unimaginable suffering for our people. Some of our neighbors had voluntarily moved west, but many more had not. Little Wolf and I managed the walk, although I often needed to carry him on my shoulders. His small legs tired easily. We are healthy. He misses you and calls out for you often. He sings the Bee Song to himself and smiles as he does so, thinking of you. But we fear that the little child, Blossom, Lula's sister, has been lost to us. So many gone. And I am sorry to tell you, but Ama did not survive."

Thomas paused, and Callie kept stone still, eyes focused on the table. She thought if she didn't move, maybe these words wouldn't, couldn't, be true. He continued.

"Sadness will haunt us for the rest of our lives. She caught a disease in one of the stopover forts, and it became impossible for her to walk. Some of our people offered her their seats in the few wagons provided to us, but she was overcome early on. There was no time to bury her, but we laid her to rest in peace under a large oak tree. We must look ahead. That is what she wanted."

Katherine started to softly cry, and Jameson's eyes were filled with tears that sat there, not quite ready to run down his cheeks. Callie still didn't move.

"In our new 'home,' and it is not yet a home, we do our best. I continue my sacred duty to lead our people in this foreign place. The United States government told us we would be paid for our things left behind, but this has not happened. Nor do we believe it will happen. We are setting up tribal governments and practicing our old ways, our dances and ceremonies. We work to make the old and the new see each other as friends, not enemies. We do what we can.

There have been many hard lessons, but we also have many strengths to help us. Above all, we must be clear about who we were and are. This is the way of the Cherokee people, and this is the way for you. We will remember. We do not give up hope to see you again.

Finally, there is something your mother wanted to tell you when you were a young woman and could understand the circumstances of your birth. She has been gone for five years, and we mourn her every day. At the same time, we thank the spirits for Little Wolf, for whom she gave her life in order to bring him into this world. It has been an honor to raise you and Little Wolf."

Thomas stopped reading and took a sip of tea before he continued.

"Even though my sister hated the man who fathered you, she chose to love you beyond words. Dove could either accept that her child had white blood or deny it. She wisely understood that you have both white and Cherokee blood. She wanted you to be proud of all of who you are.

She gave you the name Callie. Dove heard Katherine's husband call his wife Kathie and saw the playfulness and kindness in it. Your name is Kathie, said with the Cherokee accent, Callie."

Callie felt as if a sharp knife had been driven into her stomach, thinking about John Payne's dark telling of the story of her name. But a gentleness followed as a sense of pride at her mother's name choice washed over her.

Thomas continued. "Dove gave you another name, too. You are Cherokee, proud and smart. The Cherokee people would usually call you by your Cherokee name at birth, but Dove wanted to tell you your Cherokee name when you were old enough to know how you had come into this world. I didn't understand her choice of naming, but I respected it. And you were loved by all, no matter your name. She made peace with what happened to her and wanted that peace for you. Dove was like a beautiful sunrise who could chase away the night. She passed on all the goodness she had in her, to you. You were her gift, a true gift of love. And your Cherokee name reflects that."

Thomas paused, and Callie felt as if every cell in her body was on fire. She had never thought much about her name until recently. She leaned closer to Thomas.

"Your Cherokee name is Ah-yo-ka, 'one who brings joy.'"

"With great love, and we will be together again. Waya"

Callie let herself explode in tears. Her heart was swirling and swirling, falling into place. She stood and then stood up again to her full height, just as Jameson had done once to impress her. She faced the small group of people who cared about her and spoke through her tears.

"My name is *Ah-yo-ka*. I am Callie and I am *Ah-yo-ka*. I will honor my mother by living in joy. I will walk on."

She stepped out of the house into the cold, fresh air. The winter sky was a mixture of lovely grays and blues, vast and open. She knew now how to go forward. It was her own heart that would always keep her safe. She would find her way.

– 19 –
Blending

The next morning, before church, Katherine and Callie made a batch of sugar jumbles, crisp, light cookies sprinkled with sugar crystals. The first time Callie tried them, she had spat them out. She wasn't used to mouthfuls of sugar, used sparingly by the Cherokee if at all. By now, however, she had enjoyed many delicious jumbles. Plans had been made to help her rejoin her family when the weather was better. Every day, she became better at blending the past, present, and future. She understood that all of them were in her.

Thomas and Jameson had already tended to the horses in the fort's corral that morning, laying down extra straw bedding for the cold weather. Big Dog ate her oats contentedly out of a pail, and when she raised her head to take the apple Jameson held out, bits of oat stuck to the soft hairs on her nose. "This is from Callie," he said. She shook her freckled head up and down as she munched on the sweet treat.

As Katherine, Thomas, and Jameson were leaving for church, Callie said, "I will go to my home." All three stopped in their tracks and turned to look at her. She hadn't been back to her home since her family had been forced out months earlier.

"I see," said Katherine. "The settlers have not moved into Rattlesnake Springs yet because it's winter. I expect your home will not be changed much. It's cold. Take my blanket, and do you want us to go with you?" asked Katherine. Callie saw her look of concern.

"No, thank you. I will go by myself, and I have my own shawl," she said.

"If that's what you would like to do, dear," said Katherine.

Jameson looked anxiously at his mother but followed her and his father out the door. Callie went to her bedroom, slung her leather pouch across her chest, patted her necklace, and wrapped the blue wool, fringed shawl tightly around her shoulders. She had never given up wearing traditional clothes, and her long deerskin skirt and well-worn moccasin boots with red beads still kept the chill away from her legs. She walked home, slowly, at first, but then gained momentum.

As she got closer and saw her hut, she felt both excitement and fear. When she opened the door, she was greeted with familiar smells: roasted corn, tobacco, and various herbs still lived there, even after her home had been robbed of its loving owners. When she again saw the things that had been broken and tossed aside by the people who had ransacked her village, she sat down heavily on Ama's bearskin blanket. After some time, she decided her focus needed to be not on what was lost but on what remained. Not only things but mostly memories. Mohe's kindness. The Bee Song with Little Wolf. Ama's warm, rough hands and Waya's clear, powerful voice. She would remember.

Callie stood and looked around for reminders of her family and of her culture. She knew immediately she would take Ama and Waya's bearskin blankets. She picked up a small woven basket lying on the floor, overlooked by the looters. Callie had helped her grandmother dye it with blueberries. It would be an honor to give it to Katherine.

Jameson opened the door, frightening her. "Oh!" she said.

"Are you all right? Ma told me where you lived. I was worried about you. I didn't know what you would find here," he said as he hesitantly entered.

Callie smiled and watched as his eyes took in her home.

He had never been in a Cherokee house. "Some things look different but not as different as I expected," he said.

He picked up a small, delicately carved wooden pipe the looters had either missed or, more likely, didn't care about. As he examined it, a single sacred eagle feather tied to the pipe with a thin strip of leather, fluttered. "This is beautiful," he said and carefully laid it back on the table it had been resting on.

"What is 'beaut-e-fol'?" Callie asked, her head tilted in typical curiosity.

"It means, well, pretty."

He came close to Callie and faced her. Blue and brown eyes, so different and so similar. He leaned in but paused. Callie didn't hesitate and gently pulled his head close to hers. They shared a sweet kiss.

Jameson said quietly, "It means you. You are beautiful."

The End

How This Book Came To Be

Several years ago, I took a class at our local community college on the history of Indigenous Peoples in America and was asked to participate in an Honors Project. I researched original source documents and then wrote fictional scenes off what I found. While I was working on the paper, which would become this book, Callie and Jameson stopped by. Callie came to me in a dream, sweet and energetic. I knew she wanted me to tell an adventure story about her, and Jameson came to me while daydreaming. A tall, skinny teenager with scruffy blond hair, whose name was Jameson, popped into my head.

I adore Westerns like *True Grit* and *Pony* and adventures like *The Princess Bride*. When I tried to use that format, the book came to life. It is well researched, but it is also a work of fiction. Some historical license has been taken to move the plot forward. However, this story has been presented with honesty and utmost respect.

I did a great deal of research for this book, including traveling to Tennessee and walking part of the trail along the Hiawassee River. It was incredibly moving. I have joined groups/newsletters/attended lectures and powwows/read books and more to learn about the Cherokee people and the Trail of Tears events. I am humbled to have had the privilege to study this.

Acknowledgments

This book is special to me, in large part because of the people who helped me write it. First, thank you to my early beta readers who gave me great feedback as did my professor, Jonathan Pollack. And in order of working with them: My heart goes out to my mentor and writing coach, Laurie Sheer. It started with you and, more importantly, kept going because of you. One doesn't usually put an acknowledgment in a children's picture book (I have written two of them), so now I want to thank my illustrator, Karina, from Ukraine, who made the characters in the Not Really series come alive. In the middle of a war, you drew Charlie and Lisa, and they love you for it. Valerie Biel, competent, patient, and wise—created my lovely website, managed all things tech, marketer and editor extraordinaire— you have my gratitude. Christine Keleny, you made the picture books much better because of your leadership and organizational skills. I'm so glad I found Atmosphere Press with all the smart and skilled people there. And to my large and loving family, especially Derek, I'd be lost without you.

Historical Notes

While Callie and Jameson and all the other characters, except General Scott, are fictional, people like them would not be unusual at the time. For example, the first women's letter-writing campaign in America was started by women against the removal. Katherine is an example of those caring women. There were also military people and leaders against the removal like Thomas. Davy Crockett was a United States senator who spoke eloquently against the removal. General Scott led the removal with much the same attitude he has in the book. Some of his words in the book are his actual quotes.

The following are selected facts from https://americanindian.si.edu/nk360/removal/pdf/related-facts.pdf. Smithsonian. National Museum of the American Indian. Native Knowledge 360 Degrees. "Did You Know? Facts About the Removal."

- The Cherokee were not the only Indigenous People to walk a Trail of Tears. Many other tribes were forced off their land to move west including the Ho-Chunk, Potawatomi, Choctaw, Shawnee and others.

- Lawmakers didn't agree on whether to pass the Indian Removal Act. Among others, Davy Crockett, a famous frontiersman, adventurer, and Tennessee Congressman was against the removal. He said his decision would "not make me ashamed in the Day of Judgment."

- One hundred thousand Native Americans were moved off their land between 1830 and 1850, forced west to less desirable farmland and poorer hunting conditions. This gave white settlers 100 million acres of tribal land.

- Approximately four to six thousand Cherokee people from all around the country died during removal to the West Indian Territory in 1838–1839. Quatie, the wife of Chief John Ross, died of pneumonia after she gave her blanket to a sick child as they walked the long trail.

- While removal created upheaval, suffering and death, it was not the end for American Indians. They have survived and thrive as their own cultural and political groups today. They continue to fight for their land and other rights in court, stolen from them so long ago.

To learn more about The Trail of Tears or The Trail Where They Cried, ask your friendly local librarian for help finding resources. I hope you do.

Bibliography

Below are a few of the many resources I used to make this book historically accurate. If you would like to know more about the sources, please contact me through my website, nanevenson.com.

https://guides.loc.gov/indian-removal-act/digital-collections The Andrew Jackson Papers <u>Alfred Balch to Andrew Jackson, January 8, 1830</u>. A wealthy citizen wrote to President Andrew Jackson:

> Excerpt: "The removal of the Indians would be an act of seeming violence—But it will prove in the end an act of enlarged philanthropy. These untutored sons of the Forest cannot exist in a state of Independence, in the vicinity of the white man. If they will persist in remaining where they are, they may begin to dig their graves and prepare to die."

<u>https://cai.siu.edu/research/lab-archival-research/cherokee.php</u>. Center for Archeological Research. Cherokee Trail of Tears. August 25, 2023.

Edmonds, Margot and Clark, Ella E. *Voices of the Winds: Native American Legends.* Published by Castel Books, 2003, 292-298.

Hershberger, Mary. "Mobilizing Women, Anticipating Abolition: The Struggle against Indian Removal in the 1830s." The Journal of American History. Vol. 86, No.1, June 1999. Published by the Oxford University Press on behalf of the Organization of American Historians, 17-20.

Hoig, Stan. *Night of the Cruel Moon: Cherokee Removal and the Trail of Tears*. Library of American Indian History Studies. Published by Facts on File, April 1, 1996, 78.

Norgen, Jill. *Lawyers and the Legal Business of the Cherokee Republic in Courts of the United States*. Law and History Review. Vol. 10, No. 2 , Autumn, 1992. Published by the American Society for Legal History, 253.

Purdue, Theda and Green, Mikael G., University of Kentucky. *The Cherokee Removal: A Brief History with Documents*. Published by Bedford Books of St. Martin's Press, 1995, 85-91.

https://indianlaw.org/node/529: *A Sorry Saga: Obama Signs Native American Apology Resolution; Fails to Draw Attention to It*. Published by the Indian Law Resource Center/Indian Country Today, 2009.

The stories and songs are available on the internet and in books. I made up the "Bee Song."

Writing this book was an honor—and also lots of fun.

Discussion Questions for *Walk On*

How did Callie and Jameson change throughout the story?

What was the most exciting moment in the story?

How did the setting impact the characters' actions?

What were some of the interesting historical details?

What is a message or lesson you learned from this book?

What is the author saying about the importance of courage for the characters and for the Cherokee people?

Have you ever had a problem you can't solve (like the removal of the Cherokee people), but you did something that helped the situation?

About Atmosphere Press

Founded in 2015, Atmosphere Press was built on the principles of Honesty, Transparency, Professionalism, Kindness, and Making Your Book Awesome. As an ethical and author-friendly hybrid press, we stay true to that founding mission today.

If you're a reader, enter our giveaway for a free book here:

SCAN TO ENTER
BOOK GIVEAWAY

If you're a writer, submit your manuscript for consideration here:

SCAN TO SUBMIT
MANUSCRIPT

And always feel free to visit Atmosphere Press and our authors online at atmospherepress.com. See you there soon!

About the Author

NAN EVENSON is the author of two award winning children's books in her *Not Really* series. She has also had multiple short stories published and awarded. Having worked with teenagers for eighteen years has given her an appreciation of all things literature for young people. She is currently working on a middle grade/young adult historical fiction time travel novel. In addition to reading everything she can get her hands on, she enjoys time with her husband, four kids, grandchildren and their part-time rescue dog.